I0609822

NEW SPACES

AN ANTHOLOGY OF SCI-FI SHORT STORIES

New Spaces: an anthology of sci-fi short stories
© 2023 Lintusen Press
Editor: Shawn L. Bird

Published by Lintusen Press
www.LintusenPress.ca

Print ISBN: 978-1-989642-38-2
Ebook ISBN: 978-1-989642-39-9

Cover art © 2023 Swati Chavda; spaceman by kakurendo via Canva

"Alien Love" by Nancy Kilpatrick was originally published as "Demon Love" in the anthology *Demon Sex*. Masquerade Books, NY. 1997.

"Across the Dark Void" by KT Wagner was previously published in *No Spider Harmed in the Making of this Book* (anthology), Arachne Press (UK), Aug 2020 and as "Arabella and the Spiders" in *Factor Four Magazine*: Issue 4, Jan 2019.

Lintusen Press
PO Box 10019
Salmon Arm BC
Canada V1E 3B9

NEW SPACES

AN ANTHOLOGY OF SCI-FI SHORT STORIES

LINTUSEN
PRESS

For you.

You know who you are
—you who dream about stars—
who imagine beginnings, far places,
new states of being, & new spaces.

CONTENTS

TIME AFTER TIME

B.C. Deeks

There it was again. That scent. Not unpleasant. But in the wrong place. Nuala looked up from her book and scanned the living room. It was her favorite space in the house, lined with bookshelves, the tea station in one corner and woodstove in the other. She enjoyed snuggling deep into the overstuffed chair beside the window at the end of a long workday, to read a book and sip herbal tea from a china mug. The work at the Scientific Futures Avatarium fulfilled her, but, as an introvert at heart, she needed solitude to recharge.

The unknown scent wafted past her nostrils once more, bringing a mental picture of something earthy and natural to mind for an instant. Then it was gone again. Nu glanced down at the heirloom Aubusson rug tucked under the front legs of her chair. Maybe it was time to risk a professional cleaning. Her maternal grandfather had purchased the carpet on an archeology expedition over a century ago and possibly mildew was causing the odor. Best to nip that before it caused damage to the precious fibers. She'd add that to her task list for the weekend.

Two days later, the smell was stronger, except this time it permeated her office. Anxiety tightened her chest. Odd. A common smell occurring in two different locales was nothing to worry about. But in the depths of her subconscious, some thought, or memory, made her think it was important. PAY ATTENTION, it said. It wasn't exactly screaming at her to RUN, but it was definitely saying, ACT NOW!

She got up from her desk and stepped into the corridor. Most mornings, colleagues wandered the halls collaborating on projects or in search of coffee but, by the end of the week, her coworkers slipped into working from home. Especially lately.

She tapped on the door across from her own.

Steven Rafferty found humor in everything. Not surprising since he had left a gaming conglomerate to join the organization. He could joke about the color of coffee, if there was nothing else happening around them. She loved that about him.

"Come on in, Pumpkin."

She pushed open his door and looked in. "You know I hate that nickname," she said, although, in her heart, she knew that was no longer true. In school, she'd been bullied about her bright copper hair and her shy nature. He used the name in a tone that sent warmth through her.

"People will never use your real name on someone with hair that particular shade of orange." he replied, with his usual smile.

When Steve joined Nuala's project team, every day became a new adventure. She'd met him as soon as she joined the Avatarium right out of college. They clicked as friends immediately even though they were opposite in every possible way. Her small delicate build and serious nature made her the stereotypical research nerd, her specialty in biomechanical science.

He was a big man, well over six feet of taut muscle, making him stand out from their cohorts at the scientific institute. When he laughed, it boomed down the corridor and, she imagined, it rattled the windows. His long black hair fell in waves to his broad shoulders most days, but when he focused on their project, he tied it into a tail and rolled his shirt sleeves up.

Together, they planned to build a cryostasis chamber for medical treatments. Their goal was to hold a seriously ill patient in stasis for extended periods without damage to their brain cells. They were combining medical and gaming technologies in a way that had never been tried before. She dropped into the only other chair in the room. "Do you smell anything odd in my office?"

Steve pushed back from his desk, causing his chair to squawk. "Just the perfect rose scent of my favorite girl."

She waved away his comment for what it was. "You big flirt." She would never risk their friendship by changing their status beyond friends. "I'm serious. I keep smelling something weird and it worries me. I picked up the same smell at home a few days ago."

He leaned forward, concern wrinkling his brow. "Have you seen a medic? That can be a sign of an illness, right?"

"No, I don't think it's anything like that. It's bugging me, that's all." She shook her head. "Anyway. How are things going with your end of the project?"

The Cryomedic Chamber Project evolved from her doctoral thesis and led to her being hired by the Avatarium. Her original idea was to design the capsules for space travel, but the Director had seen a medical opportunity by combining her space concept with gaming technology.

The project had a simple premise: rest the body so it could heal while keeping the brain active and healthy. Their hypothesis was that allowing the subconscious to remain fully active while the conscious mind was dormant would ensure that no damage occurred, no matter how long the treatment period was. Her part was the chamber that would hold the patient's body in stasis for as long as was needed to cure the illness, thereby removing all superfluous demands on the patient's autonomic body functions. Steve's helmet design, evolved from virtual gaming technology, would engage the patient's brain so that it didn't deteriorate over the treatment period. Long term inactivity was known to damage brain cells related to memory and other functionality.

Steve settled back in his chair again. "I sent our virtual reality design for the helmet down to the development team to build a prototype this morning. The Director approved the design this time. I copied you on the final submission."

"I know you were disappointed with the delay after he rejected the last one, but we can't mess around with something that connects to the human brain."

Steve sighed. "We've got it this time, though."

This latest upgrade was for a memory component. The solution had hit them while watching an iconic old movie late one night about astronauts travelling through space while their mind relived the required time span of actual life memories. A year of space travel between planets felt like no time had passed if they simply re-lived their previous year in their mind. They ran with the idea by programming their helmet to tap into their patient's memory to pass their time in stasis.

Nu scanned Steve's face and noticed new lines and

shadows around his eyes. Tension creased his brow, and his skin was drawn and pale as if he'd been pulling all-nighters lately. He'd rolled up the sleeves of his jean shirt and the muscles of his forearms flexed as he laced his fingers together on the top of his desk. She pulled in a deep breath and sighed. "What's bothering you, Steve? It isn't like you to be so glum."

"I'm afraid we're running out of time, Nu."

She sat up straighter. "What do you mean?"

"I have a friend in Virology at the Federal Medical Center," he said. "The pandemic is spreading, and each variation is worse than the last."

Nuala tilted her head and frowned. "That's the way viruses behave—they mutate and adapt. The restrictions are having an impact."

"Have you heard the talk about a Fifth Wave?"

"Of course, but this time, they're clamping down and will get it all under control."

"They are trying to clamp down. But they can't do it."

"We have vaccinations that are working. We just have to get them out."

"It's taking too long," Steve said, shaking his head. "And the variants are mutating faster than we can cope. The current vaccine doesn't even cover this latest variant."

"So far," Nuala said, dropping her gaze from his. "But the scientists will figure it out. They have so far."

The global pandemic had started small; a pocket of the virus had erupted in a small city in Asia sixteen months before. Within four months, it spread around the world, killing millions of people. A vaccination had been announced within a year, but the distribution was slow and difficult.

Finally, Steve shrugged and chuckled. "I'm letting it get to me."

That worried her because Steve never let anything get to him. Even a global pandemic.

She didn't have time to consider their conversation because the Director shortened the deadline on their project the next day.

The helmet prototype lay dead center on her desk. She looked up at her friend and smiled. "It works?"

"Like the piece of genius it is intended to be." Steve's grin spread from ear to ear.

"I knew you could do it."

"It's intimidating when you're messing with brain matter. Somehow, it's no longer a game."

"It's still just tech, Steve. And you are a tech genius. How did the test go?"

"Amazing." He beamed. "The patient wore the helmet for an entire surgery. No pain even though they didn't use medications, and since his brain believed there was no trauma to his body at all, his recovery time was reduced."

"The body believes what the brain tells it."

"Exactly. An altered reality."

"You do amazing work, big guy."

"Now it's time for you to do your amazing work, little one. Can you integrate it with your capsule design?"

"Already did. I knew you'd iron out the problems. Now it's just plug and play."

"Without the plug." He laughed and straightened to his full height. "Gotta love solar power. So, we're good to go?"

She nodded and saw his shoulders visibly shed the weight of worry.

She stepped back and around the desk. "Steve, talk to me. What's gotten into you? Is there something you aren't telling me?" She leaned her butt onto the edge of her desk and motioned him to sit.

He settled into her visitor chair while she boosted herself up on her desktop.

"I've been hanging out in some of the underground chat rooms," he said.

She leaned forward, clutching the edge of the desk. "You're being careful? You'll lose your job if they catch you there."

He crossed his arms over his chest. "They won't, and I need to find out what's going on. There're too many platitudes on the news with no real progress on rolling out the vaccinations."

"Politics are always a load of crap, Steve. It doesn't mean the world is coming to an end."

"Usually, I'd agree with you. But there are too many little things. I couldn't shake the uneasy feelings."

"The vaccination does work. Don't get caught up in the conspiracy theories about a hoax," she said, afraid the stress of their long work hours might have pulled him down that rabbit hole.

He shook his head. "It's not that. That is rampant paranoia. But it's like I said. All the little things."

She leaned back on her hands. And because he was a really smart guy, she said, "Okay, go through it for me."

He huffed out a breath and then raised his big hand and started to count off his concerns one at a time. "First, the vaccinations do work, but the supply is limited and the roll out too slow. Two, the health professionals are pushing up against the politicians so they can't get the restrictions implemented effectively or adapt them as quickly as the virus is changing."

"But the vaccination is working on the variants because they are all the one root virus," she interrupted him, wanting to be sure he kept to the facts. "We haven't seen a single new virus."

"That is true," he agreed. "However—"

He raised a third finger, "—pandemic fatigue is

spreading with more demonstrations every day. More resistance among the population refusing to comply with the restrictions."

It was her turn to nod. That was also a fact.

"That's what's causing the Fifth Wave, Nu. If people won't comply with the restrictions, it could tip the balance."

Nu stared at him. "You think they'll refuse to get the vaccination?"

"I'm not a virus specialist, but it's such a complex balance. The friend I told you about tried to explain it to me, but all I understood is that the rate of virus spread balances against the rate of vaccination. Humanity is in trouble unless a natural immunity develops or that balance is maintained."

"Aren't you being a bit apocalyptic, Steve? We aren't anywhere near that point yet."

"That's the big question," Steve said. "Perhaps we are. How would we know? It's not like there'll be some big announcement. It will keep creeping up on us until one day, it tips."

Those words played through her mind over the following days, impossible to accept but too important to reject. How long might it take for a virus to wipe out humanity? Surely, they were talking decades. There would be warnings. Governments all over the world would take steps.

Right?

She spent the following weekend cleaning her living room from top to bottom, throwing open the windows to air out the house like her grandmother used to do in the old days. Spring was in the air and with it came a promise of new life. And the end of the pandemic, she hoped. They were still in lock down so she couldn't have friends over for a coffee or go out for dinner. It was horrifying to think how long it would take for the economy to recover from the impact of restrictions on local business.

The pandemic moved into its second year. And as everyone was forced into isolation, market demands encouraged the Avatarium to make further modifications to the Cryomedic Capsules beyond professional medical purposes. People were bored and wanted something to occupy their minds and to convince their bodies that they were living fulfilling lives. Nu's project team created advanced programming to compensate for the physical and mental implications of restrictions that limited the contact people could have with their loved ones, especially with travel prohibited.

Once she and Steve worked out the basic parameters, they continued to develop programming that allowed people to communicate with each other from the capsules, then attend educational institutions remotely from within the units. Owners could even personalize the capsules with their names. Production could hardly keep up with demand.

The only glitch that Nu continued to struggle with was that earthy, not quite unpleasant smell. Darn it. It permeated everything she did, but she seemed to be the only one who picked up on it. With the demands of the project, she didn't have time to take Steve's advice to get a medical assessment. The virus did not affect scent and she knew she was otherwise healthy. She had to ignore the smell for now—until after this crisis. When she wasn't so busy. After all, it wasn't unpleasant. Just unexplained.

Then, one day, as she was in her office talking to Steve about another upgrade to the capsules, she heard it. CLICK. HIIISSSS.

"Steve?"

"Yes?" She'd interrupted him mid-sentence. He cocked an eyebrow.

"What was that sound?"

"What sound?" As he spoke, her vision blurred. His body faded. The walls were no longer smooth grey paint but dull, metallic.

"Steve?" Panic cramped her muscles and her voice shot up several octaves. The lights dimmed and everything around her waned. She squeezed her eyes shut and sucked in a deep breath. That damn smell. Earthy, Dank. It was overpowering now. Maybe she did have a brain tumor. She should have gotten a medical assessment, like Steve said. She pulled in more air. It was moist, gritty, and she choked. Was she having a seizure of some kind? A stroke?

She waited a moment longer, certain that she would feel her friend's arms around her any second as she regained consciousness. But nothing happened.

Awareness seeped through her panic. She was lying on a cushioned, soft surface, not the hard floor. She wiggled her toes, then her fingers. She lifted her eyelids, but it was too dark to make out where she was. She squeezed her fingers into a fist, but every movement was sluggish. She blinked a few times, trying to clear her sight. Figure out where she was. She reached up a hand and bumped into something firm. Pushed it away.

Gradually, her eyes adjusted to the filtered light, and she scanned her surroundings. She covered her mouth with both hands and screamed.

Dark green foliage wove through the remains of a window to her right and beyond that were trees with intermittent slivers of cerulean blue sky. She heard panting breath and realized it was her own. She took a slow deep breath, let it out. Another. And another. Now wasn't the time to pass out. Her heart rate slowed, and her spinning senses settled. She squinted around her, allowing her mind to catch up with what she was seeing, and confirmed her fear. She was lying in one of her Cryomedic Capsules. But why? Had she suffered a medical crisis? Maybe it was just a bad test. Or she had a seizure, and they had to put her in a medical coma. She looked up at the twining vines hanging over her, then slowly stretched up and touched the nearest one. A shower of moisture rained down on her, rousing her scrambled brain.

She swiped the water off her face and struggled to sit up. With one more deep inhalation to fortify her courage, she gazed out from her position. More dense greenery stretched out over building ruins in three directions. In the distance, a ribbon of water twisted through a forest of trees, winding its way between familiar mountain ridges. The sun sat halfway between two peaks—heading down or up, she couldn't be sure.

In her immediate vicinity, the sunlight bounced off a dozen or more capsules. Another scream fought to break through, but she fought it, forcing her mind to assess the pods nearest her until she found it. STEVEN RAFFERTY etched on the side of one. Seeing it, her breath whooshed out of her as a sob. She hugged her knees to her chest and dug into her mind for remnants of memory.

Smell first. That earthy scent she'd been picking up for days, weeks. The surrounding forest had been seeping into her resting place as the seal on her capsule deteriorated. How much time she couldn't be sure, but decades, at least. Once it lost integrity, the capsule released her. A failsafe she'd designed to prevent someone from being trapped and suffocating.

Glancing at the pods around her, she shook her head. What were they all doing trapped in the capsules? These weren't all accidents. Or surgeries. Then she remembered her final conversation with Steve.

The pandemic was out of control. Governments did not have the means to rein in the virus and now it would have to run its course. The order had come down from the Director to repurpose the Avatarium's capsules as escape pods ... not to outer space, but to cryostasis. Their final enhancement had been a simple one; the memory loop coded to continuously stimulate the mind to prevent degradation. In theory, an entire lifetime could be re-lived, if necessary—time after time after time, for as long as the body was held in cryostasis—because they didn't know how long a killing virus would last. There was no time to retrofit the pods with timers or special features for the emergency. The final solution was to lock yourself in a cryostasis capsule if you have one to wait out the virus, re-living your life in a memory loop, and HOPE for a future.

Nuala scanned the encroaching forest and the misty horizon hugging the distant mountains. How long had she and the others waited? What did this new future have in store for them? With the seal damaged, her pod was no longer usable. The other units were at the end of their life cycle, too. It was time to move forward.

She struggled out of her capsule and held on to the side while her leg muscles remembered how to hold her upright. Then she took a step towards the pod with the familiar name on its side, STEVEN RAFFERTY. At least she wouldn't be facing this new world alone.

Author **B.C. Deeks** writes heartwarming stories of mystery and magic. In her action-packed fantasy adventure series, BEYOND THE MAGIC, mythics and mortals band together to battle dark magic and overthrow a corrupt Council in a quest to defeat an ancient prophecy. Born and raised in Newfoundland (Canada), she currently lives in Alberta. Find BC Deeks' news at www.bcdeeks.com.

A NEW EARTH

Finnian Burnett

"First class to the left," Bonnie says automatically, bored already as she takes passes and pushes first-class passengers along. "Don't hold up the line." Many of them, the first-class ones, push their passes at her without sparing her a glance.

"Economy to the right," she says, waving a smiling family unit to the lift for the lower decks. No windows below, no decorations, either. She wonders for a moment how long their excited anticipation will last in the dimly lit halls below. Still.

"Enjoy your trip," she calls after them.

They wave back at her, still smiling as the lift doors

close. Their faces stay with her, many of them. Hopeful, anxious. Brave people looking to escape the ravages of their home planet. She wants to hug all the lower decks passengers, to tell them the journey will be bad, but the reward will be worth it.

Bonnie has been working the Earth emigration ships for ten years and they've barely made a dent in the population. Still, at least the system is fairer than she'd expected when she had first been hired by the company. Rich and poor alike can book passage, and no one in the lower decks has to pay for their travel. Though, of course, the rich get better accommodations.

It's a six-month journey and people who can afford to pay for the luxury of room, spread out over the upper decks, with holographic picture windows and double-sized cabins and separate storage units into which they've paid extra to cram their paintings and electronics and bags of gold.

Bonnie sighs and accepts another bunch of pass-holders. This time, it's a group of scientists, climate change activists who'd done their best in the last few years to save the planet before deciding to leave for the new one. She waves them down to the lower decks. No room for middle-class on immigration ships—just long rows of economy bunks, each with a trunk bedside for the one piece of carry-on luggage each passenger is permitted to bring.

The scientists smile and chat with Bonnie while waiting for the lift. She offers to meet them later in the lower decks mess hall. *Bound to be a great conversation at that table*.

During a break in the line, Bonnie watches a crane lift a pallet of belongings onto the upper decks. She grins. A couch, for Christ's sake. Someone is bringing a couch into space? She's still laughing when a family approaches and the youngest, a child of maybe four, hands her the passes with trembling hands.

"Will we see aliens on the ship?" he asks her, wonder in his voice.

Bonnie crouches in front of him, smiling. "We are the aliens now," she says. "But," she continues, patting him on the head, "when we round the argon nebula, I'll make sure to point out the planet where the Torrexcians live. They're our new friends."

The child grins and rushes toward the lift with his family. Lower decks, of course. It would be an uncomfortable six months, but the reward of their new home at the end of the journey would make it worthwhile.

Two men in three-piece suits clomp up the ramp, cookie-cutter wives a few steps behind. "I must protest that there isn't a separate entrance for first class," one of them says as soon as he reaches Bonnie's station. He stares back at the line, a disdainful sneer curling his lip. "I've been standing in line with *these people* for hours."

These people. Bonnie looks out over the hundreds of people still in line—families, workers, teachers, librarians. Some people carry nothing but a beloved book or stuffed animal. Most are exhausted and hungry by the time they make it to the ship, but everyone gets a meal once aboard and no one will starve on New Earth.

One of the wives clutches a tiny dog. Bonnie reaches for it.

"All pets go to the lower decks," she says. "We'll take good care of them there."

"Boo-boo stays with me," the wife says, pouting, and though Bonnie's orders were to give the wealthy whatever they asked for, on this subject, she puts her foot down. "All pets go to lower decks. We don't have the capacity to care for them on the upper decks."

The woman opens her mouth to protest, but the ship's security is there. The woman looks into the stern face of the uniformed guards and thrusts her pet toward Bonnie. "You better take care of her," she says, and turns away. Bonnie hands the little dog over to one of the guards, resisting the urge to kiss its fuzzy head. "Take it down to the kennels."

Most passengers don't raise a fuss over giving up their pets for the duration, but some do. Animals need special considerations to be safe in space and the staff can't do that if the pets are scattered throughout private cabins. Besides, Bonnie thinks, giving the woman her most ingratiating company smile, pets have a much better time in the lower decks, even separated from their owners. Bonnie herself often visits the pet area to make sure all the animals are treated right. In her previous life, she'd worked at a shelter, and she still loves dogs and cats more than most people. Bonnie doesn't bother to reassure the woman, but the dog will be well cared for, fed, and watered. Like the people on the lower decks, the dogs won't have much space, but they'll be tended and treated well, and they'll be happy to run free in the wild grasses of New Earth at the end of the journey.

The two men, oil executives, according to their passes,

take their wives' arms and head for the upper deck lift. She watches the lift door close behind them. The hugely inflated cost to make the voyage on the upper deck is more than most people make in their lifetimes. The money funds climate change and world hunger programs on old Earth, but it also covers the energy needed for the round-trip immigration. On New Earth, they don't need money. Everyone works as they can, everyone has equal access to food, medicine, housing.

A woman approaches shyly and hands her pass to Bonnie. "I almost didn't make my taxi on time," she says, and her voice is so pleasant, Bonnie stares. The woman's face is glowing, thrilled. She looks all around the ship, the doors to the lift, at Bonnie herself. "I couldn't find my toothbrush and I didn't know if they'd have any onboard. I'm so excited," the woman says. "I'm sorry I'm babbling." She smiles. "My name is Jenna."

Jenna is dressed casually in jeans and what looks like a handknit sweater. She's carrying a backpack and nothing else. Lower decks, for sure. Bonnie likes her already and can't wait to get to know her during the long hours ahead of them. Bonnie scans Jenna's pass and frowns. Upper decks. It can't be. She scans it again. The woman is a librarian, Bonnie reads on the scanner. "Upper decks?" Bonnie almost chokes on the words.

The woman smiles again. She meets Bonnie's eyes; her gaze is soft and kind. Bonnie wants to grab her, throw her in the lower deck's lift. This woman does not belong on the upper decks. "How did you..." Bonnie pauses, not sure how to ask the question.

"How did a librarian get to the upper decks?" The woman laughs. "We wanted to make sure all our favorite books were going to New Earth. So, when the lottery pulled my name to make the trip, most of the libraries on the planet donated to pay for my passage."

"You can petition to have certain books taken in cargo," Bonnie says. "You didn't have to pay for the upper deck passage."

"This way, we'll never have to worry about a shortage of books." She shrugs, looking sheepish. "I know your company is doing your best. But I don't know. I guess we wanted to make sure nothing was left behind."

The company has digitally scanned every book to date and they update the collection every time they come back to Earth. This woman, all her colleagues, what had they given up to bring a storage bay worth of paper books to their new planet? Bonnie stares down at the scanner, frantically thinking. She can't let this kind woman go among the vultures in the upper decks. "Listen," she says. "Your room isn't ready yet. I'm going to send you down to the lower decks just to wait. I'll come get you when it's ready."

The woman looks at Bonnie with trusting eyes. "Okay. Thank you."

From the lower decks, passengers can't access the upper decks without a pass. When the lift doors close on the woman, Bonnie keys in a new designation, lifting the upper deck privileges from the librarian. Later, Bonnie will find her in the mess hall and explain. Somehow, she'll try to make her understand.

Tonight, on the ship, the upper-class passengers will talk about how they're going to take over when they get to New Earth, and put some order back into the socialist nightmare Bonnie's company has created. She's heard it hundreds of times. Rumors have filtered back to Earth about the social order of New Earth and a lot of people make the trip just to change the way things are. Tonight, they'll tell her all about it when she stops in to bring them a complimentary bottle of champagne and chocolate-covered strawberries.

Bonnie just smiles and lets them have their dreams. They spread out on the upper decks, drink their free champagne, and barely spare a thought for the poor folks down in the lower decks, crammed into the bunks below.

They have it so good, Bonnie thinks, grinning to herself. But she'd been working on this ship since the early days, and she was there when the elderly billionaire from that online shopping company froze to death as they passed the third moon of Regulas Major.

The ship's engines keep the lower decks warm, too warm, maybe, but no one had ever frozen to death on the lower decks. No one ever died of asphyxiation on the lower decks, either, like four upper-decks people did when a bulkhead broke open on Bonnie's second flight. A class action lawsuit disappeared. In space, no one can hear you scream and that goes double for lawyers.

After the first couple of years, it became more expedient to simply dump the upper decks once the ship got far enough away from Earth. Less fuel, nicer people. The new planet was shaping up fine. Another three years of service, and Bonnie would settle there herself, riding on the lower decks, of course. Perhaps she'd adopt a dog.

The line moves on and Bonnie directs people to their appropriate stations. A leering man pinches her butt as he passes and Bonnie fakes a smile. "How about a free upgrade to first class," she says. "A cabin has just opened."

Finnian Burnett teaches undergrad creative writing and English. They've published several novels, but their true love is flash fiction. Their flash collection, *The Clothes Make the Man*, was recently released by Ad Hoc Publishing. In their spare time, Finnian watches a lot of *Star Trek* and takes their cat for walks in a stroller.

THE OBERRAN MYCELIUM

Andrew G. Cooper

Alva touched down in a sea of tall, purple grass-like tendrils, rolled, and slammed into the ground. She laid on her back, dazed, staring into Oberran's swirling orange and rosy sky. A low moan escaped her lips. Fourth time's a charm. She unclipped her landing gear and stood up stiffly. Thank the void for the low gravity on this moon.

Spindly crimson bushes punctured the field of violet grass that acted as a landing site. Alva inhaled, filling her lungs from her suit's oxygen canisters, and let out a long, slow breath. A circle of condensation fogged up part of the visor's interior Heads-Up Display—the HUD, she had to remember their fancy acronyms. Turning slowly, she searched through the numbers, gauges, and lights on the inside of her helmet until she found her target. A forest, if you could call it that, of towering tree-mushrooms grew like a wall nearby. Right on target. Oberran was a beautiful and haunting moon—totally alien from the green-covered Orthial Alva called home—but she didn't want to be anywhere else in the system. Especially now. Especially after—no, she wouldn't think of them now.

Airborne spore clusters floated by on a breeze Alva couldn't feel from the confines of her ExtraVehicular Activity suit. The little seed-like structures glowed dimly in the morning sky as they danced out of the fungi forest. The tranquility was almost staggering. It was so good to be back.

Wrrrrrshhhhh!

Alva turned as another sleek black EVA suit landed nearby—much more gracefully than she had, of course. The HUD rangefinder readout next to the anemometer put it at eighty-seven metres. That would be Altair Regulus, of course. Sure enough, the NovaGen agent strode through the grass a minute later, moving with the unmistakable ease of one familiar with low g environments.

"This path leads to where the drones scouted last,"

Altair said over the comms in way of a greeting. It wasn't a question, and his matter-of-fact voice was as flat and precise as a razor.

Alva nodded with her fist in response. "Satellites and drones pinpointed the epicentre to somewhere in this dense structure." She turned and strode towards the stalks of the gigantic fungi. Any excuse not to be looking at Altair's stupid face.

"Well, let's hope you're right, yah. For everyone's sake," he replied.

Alva hated the refined, corporate way Altair spoke. It was characteristic of Artanans, and it grated her. She reminded herself that she needed NovaGen to complete her research and so she needed "Agent Regulus" as well. She really didn't think of herself as xenophobic, especially against mooners, but jerks were jerks. Anyway, she knew the game. She always put on a smiling face.

Thick tendrils rustled around her thighs as Alva stepped under the canopy of mushroom caps. A strange sensation, like something watching her, prickled the back of her neck. She shook her head inside her helmet.

Not now. She needed to focus today.

"Stay within eyesight," she said, wading through the

underbrush. "It's going to be a labyrinth in here."

A gentle green glow from the fungoid gills above was the only thing that punctuated the darkness now. The bioluminescent luciferins they produced were on Alva's list of future research possibilities. Of course, there would never be enough time to tackle all the items on that ever-growing list. There never was.

Alva scanned through the swirls of flitting spores before her. Nothing abnormal showed on the HUD. It was so quiet in this deep place. This was one of the greatest wonders of Lavaria's moons. Her pulse quickened slightly. She felt momentarily rooted to the spot, like she herself was sending out hyphae through the dense, black soil beneath her boots.

"How do you know where we're going?" Altair's voice asked in her helmet.

Alva realized she'd stopped and checked the device on her suit's wrist. They were on course, according to the screen. "I don't," she replied. "We're following the best guess based on surveillance data."

"But you did find traces of a new genus, Doctor Anastis?"

"The local lab found traces of new organic compounds spread across this region in unprecedented numbers. We're following those to what we hope is their source."

"The new spores, yah," Altair prompted. After she didn't respond, he continued. "I read your report. Thoroughly."

The underbush was growing thinner now, and smaller, knee-high mushrooms with gold and orange caps littered the forest floor. Alva was careful not to touch any of the creeping vines that crawled up the tall fungi as she navigated between their stems. She checked her HUD. Her heart rate had returned to normal, but there were no other changes.

"In a manner of speaking," she finally replied. "It seems the spore clusters are growing thicker the deeper we go into the forest. We'd have to take measurements to be sure, but make sure to monitor your air filters."

The corporate agent said something in a language Alva didn't understand then barked a harsh laugh. "I suppose you wouldn't need to worry about that. What with your bioimplants? A respiration compounder gland, yah, yah?"

Alva stopped and turned back. Her suit immediately identified her companions' location. Good thing, too. The dim green light barely reflected off the black suit twenty metres behind her.

"As I noted, I read your report." It was so hard to guess

at tones in his voice. It sounded vaguely threatening.

"I'm glad NovaGen has been so thorough on this project," she said coolly before returning to the path she was forging.

"NovaGen is very careful with its assets," came the reply in her helmet.

Of course it was. Alva knew only too well. Her first trip to this strange, foreign world had been a critical success. It had ensured her doctorate with honours, creating an uproar around her thesis publication. That first discovery—which had given the biotech industry a monumental boost—put her on the map at Charlock University and had ensured her numerous prestigious offers in the mycology industry after graduation. Unfortunately, subsequent trips to the outer system hadn't garnered nearly as exciting results. Now NovaGen was threatening to pull funding on the extremely expensive expeditions unless another meaningful discovery was made. Not that it mattered much to her anymore.

This was her fourth, and final, time on this moon. Whether or not she was successful, Doctor Alva Anastis knew she would not be coming back. She had been able to outrun nearly every problem in her life before, but not this one. This time was different. She loved field work, even with the high risks (and higher costs), but she knew it was sometimes just an excuse to escape home for months at a time. It was hard to explain to her partner. Sometimes she just needed to be away, to get out, to get off Orthial and into the wide expanses. Sometimes she just needed space. And this eerie, beautiful place drew her back time and time again.

She told herself she wasn't escaping from anything but that she was escaping towards some…thing. The soft glow of bioluminescence. The beautifully complex flora. The multiplicity of an Oberran sunset. And that…feeling. Like a fingertip brushing against an exposed wound, it tugged at her mind. A fog pressing into her senses. She wished she could get out of this voiding suit and really experience this forest. She hadn't laid through twelve hours of surgery getting these implants for nothing. But there were protocols to follow. NovaGen management loved their protocols.

The change happened gradually, so it took some time for the Alva to notice. Her mind had wandered, but she did notice. The thing that tipped her off was the spores. They were definitely thicker now, swirling above the rippling river of purple tendrils like swarms of insects. Even in the darkness of the forest, they glowed with strange halos of light—like the dancing lumos lights of ancient Orthialian lore. And there was more. A mould the hue of fire clung to surfaces all around her. She leaned closer to inspect. Stems, plants, the ground, even her suit had particles on it, like a faint dusting of rust shifting in the wind. She closed her eyes and shook her head.

"We've stopped, yah," came the voice in her ear.

Alva's wrist device showed they were much deeper now and getting closer to the centre. She glanced at the readout on the interior of her helmet's visor. Something was wrong.

"There's something ahead," she said. "The wind's picking up."

"What is it?"

Gusts pushed against Alva's suit and wafts of spores flew by. "I don't know, but it's heading our way fast." She checked the readouts again. "If we get caught off guard in low g, we m—"

A wall of wind. The shout of a tempest. Alva hit the ground.

The forest transformed into a murky river of gold and orange, plunging her into its depths.

"Mould!" she yelled into her mic. "Spores and—"

She was drowning in a mould storm, unable to see even

a metre past her visor.

"Come—oct—Anas..." Altair's chittering, distorted voice cut in and out. "I can't—er—...do—copy?"

Alva rolled to the stem of a nearby tree-mushroom and watched as the mould ate through the leafy vines clinging there. The rate of decomposition staggered her. Icy cold seeped through her face. Her stomach tightened. Alva twisted frantically until the green crosshairs that signified Altair's location appeared on the HUD. Southwest. She couldn't see him through the blasting winds, but dragged herself in that direction nonetheless. A dozen metres. If she could just get close enough...

WHAM!

Pain smashed into Alva's back with a crack and a grunt. Something grabbed her wrist. She instinctively rolled away.

"Anastis! By the Darkness, I thought..." It was Altair. They were close enough that their comms were working.

"It's a mould storm.," she rasped, trying to catch her breath. "A really bad one. I've never heard of anything close to this volume."

Alva propped herself into a seated position. Her companion's faceplate came into view and she focused on his dark eyes, wide with what must be fear.

"How long, yah?" he asked. Seeing the sweat across his forehead made Alva recognized she was perspiring too.

"Could be minutes. Maybe hours. If it goes too long, the mould will eat through organic material, rotting it away."

"Void me—what?!"

"Our suits are synthetic," Alva replied. "Should be fine. We can move for—"

Altair shook her by the shoulder, his face red. "We have to turn back, yah? You said the air filters won't hold, and we can't comm with the lab from here."

An aching spasm shot down Alva's back. "We have to continue. If we turn back now we won't make it to the centre." She tasted iron as she closed her eyes and shook her head.

"I'm in charge here, yah? I say when we're turning back." The shifting gold light of the storm gave Altair's furrowed expression a haunted cast.

"We don't know how long the fungi bloom will last. This is a once in a lifetime opportunity." Alva pushed herself to her feet, staying low in the fungoid whirlwind. "I have to move forward. I won't be coming back."

"Don't be so noble, Doctor Asteris." Altair was nothing but a disembodied voice again.

"I'm not being noble, I have t—"

"Then don't be so voiding stubborn, yah!" he barked.

Alva grit her teeth. She'd turned her back on so many things recently. She'd run away from…well, from everything.

"I'm going ahead," she said simply. "Head back to the lab if you want."

She turned into the storm, grabbed a handful of purple tendrils, and took one low step after another.

"That was a command, Doctor Asteris. Are you…I—fine! You'll have a deluge of documents to—when you return, yah! If you return…"

His voice crackled as a force seemed to pull Alva into the depths of Oberran's wilderness. Static garbled through her helmet speakers, and suddenly she was entirely alone on an alien moon. For all the good her comms were, she could have been at the bottom of an ocean. Or on another planet entirely. She felt farther from people than she ever had, even after leaving her family over six million kilometres behind.

It was isolating. It was liberating.

No more worried glances from Branderan. No more heavy sighs from Larissa. Alva fought onwards, clinging, crawling, and pushing through the swirling fog of spores.

Time slipped away.

She travelled for five minutes or perhaps fifty. No, it

must have been over an hour. Her muscles ached all over, a dull soreness throbbing through her, but each step grew easier. Her heart rate still read over triple its resting, according to the HUD. Her suit's oxygen level lowered steadily, though not to the point where she should be concerned…yet. She may have been right about the air filters though, they were in the red. But the wind only tugged at her now. More and more tree-mushroom stems emerged through the gloom as the air cleared. Spores still swamped her. They seemed omnipresent, but when Alva looked up to the canopy ceiling, the gentle glow of the gills reached the forest floor again. The storm had passed. She knew what to do.

Alva inhaled and held her breath. External temperature read twelve degrees centigrade. The HUD lights flashed crimson as she unclipped and unscrewed her helmet. Everything in the suit screamed for her to not take it off, but take it off she did. Oberran's brisk breeze caressed her, instantly cooling her clammy face. Her lungs bristled. The helmet slipped from Alva's gloves and clanked to the ground. She released her breath and air, thick and fragrant, rushed into her lungs and inflated her chest.

The sharp scent of moss, mould, and soil filled the mycologist's nose. After the stifling confines of her suit, the cool air felt sweet and fresh and fine. She breathed in, feeling her bioimplants activating. Rich carbon dioxide coursed through the throat gland and across the nodules on her lungs. She felt elated breathing real air again.

A stinging stab yanked at Alva's mind. Where it had been a tickle while inside her helmet, now a fist scraped inside her skull. White and gold spots dotted her vision. Her hands vibrated with a mucid chill.

She could see the way forward.

The spores. It was hard to believe they ever seemed like random floating specks. The clusters swirled and rolled in the breeze as before, but now Alva could see the pattern in them. Circles, spirals, and geometric waves flowed through the air all around—so clearly, so vividly, pointing the way. Just like the dancing lights her grandmother had told her about that led deeper into the enchanted forest. Alva stepped forward and the entire forest pulsed with gold light as the glow of the spores expanded. The helmet of the EVA suit laid abandoned at the base of a tree-mushroom, forgotten.

Alva moved as if in a dream now. Not in the timeless haze of the storm but in a flowing movement of delight. Each step was a step towards her destination. Each step felt right. It grew brighter and brighter as she approached what she now knew to be the true centre of this forest—though forest wasn't the right word anymore. She was heading towards the heart. To the core. Where were these sensations coming from? She didn't care. For the first time since her diagnosis, she felt hopeful.

The foliage parted suddenly into a clearing as Alva pushed through a wall of crimson bushes and purple tendrils. She gasped. A gigantic fungoid structure towered in the open space before her. It unfurled upwards like a multicoloured flower in bloom, easily as large as a full-grown oak. Thick, bark-like chiton covered its stems and branches, creating the effect of a many-trunked tree crossed with kraken tentacles punching upwards from the ground. The branches—limbs?—waved gently as if sensing its surroundings, each pulsing with lines of emerald and violet lights.

Alva was dimly aware her mouth hung agape as she reached her arms towards the pulsating giant before her. Everything had led her to this moment. With stunning clarity, she understood that now. Not just this trip, or her research, but her whole life. Each choice she ever made had inevitably and irrevocably led her to where she now stood.

She was taking her gloves off as she stumbled and jumped through the low gravity, then her hand was against the base of the great being before her. A presence blasted into her mind, and she knew the thing she was touching was alive. They were intelligent. Their sentience, their very being, was as vast as an ocean and she sunk into it with the rapturous descent of falling in love.

In that moment, Alva saw herself. She smelled the pores on the nape of her neck. She heard the teflon and kevlar fabric of her EVA suit's outer layer as she shifted. She felt the heat radiating from her hands and head. She couldn't see, not in a literal sense, but she could detect herself completely.

Alva let go and was pulled down deep.

The true body of the being lay beneath the earth. It started at her feet and expanded in every direction through an immense mycelium network. The giant tree-mushrooms surrounding her were simply fruiting bodies. The million tendrils of those grass-like plants were tiny fingers sensing the surface of the planet—each one a hypha spanning kilometres underground from the central core. This entire forest, dozens of kilometres across, was one living, breathing, feeling being.

All fungi are closer to animals than to plants, of course, but this was different. This being was beyond humanity's comprehension. Human preoccupation with intelligence, phyla, species, sexes, and genders could not fathom the multiplicity of this being. Alva smiled. She had grown tired of fitting into categories her whole life—of the pressure from her immigrant parents to excel as a scientist. She was given the opportunity to live on a green and blue planet with breathable air, and she was expected to use that advantage to make her family proud. They never understood why she needed bioimplants. Why would she want to breathe on another world, in another atmosphere? Why would she want to leave paradise? She'd taken a step towards transhumanism. She just didn't fit anywhere. But in the presence of this being, she felt like perhaps she didn't need to.

Alva's fingers grasped tighter, squeezing the chitinous stem as an ancient presence plunged into her mind. She didn't feel thoughts or words, but impulses washed over her. The connection was unlike anything she had ever felt before. It surpassed the passionate, burning desire she'd felt for Larissa when they started dating. What was this sensation? It surpassed simple emotions. She saw how miniscule she was, just one tiny human among billions clinging to the surface of one moon among hundreds in a single solar system that was itself one of thousands of millions in the galaxy. And at the same time, she was expansive, connected to this boundless intelligence.

She felt the spores inside her. Filtered through her lungs. Swimming through her veins. Brushing her brain stem. She was a galaxy—linked to the great family of life. Her loved ones, all of humanity. Everything from rodents and reptiles, to the dreamers of Lavaria's skies and miniscule extremophiles of asteroids. This being of Oberran. They were brothers, mothers, and grandparents all at once.

This truth settled into Alva's body. It was so simple, yet so profound that her bones shook with the weight of it. She was alive. She was a life.

"It's terminal," the doctor had said what seemed like a lifetime ago. She could see the dark skin of his creased face as clearly now as when he had been standing in front of her. "Our suspicions were, unfortunately, correct. It is the same disease that took your mother."

Alva had rebelled. She had fled. She ran away and had been running ever since.

Larissa's face materialized before her, crowned in gold light . Pain pooled in those beautiful eyes. Alva didn't want that pain. She didn't want any of it.

"We can get through this together," Larissa's voice swam around her. "We can get through anything. I won't leave you."

And she hadn't. But Alva did.

Her partner disappeared in a wisp of light.

Branderan whispered and Alva turned to see him standing behind her, wreathed in a golden glow. "You won't find what you're looking for out there," her brother had said to her. "Even if you find the cure. What you're looking for is already here." Then he disappeared, just another memory buried into the past.

The being stretched deeper through time than Alva thought possible. They were millenia old, with collections of memories spanning lives across the entire moon. Her own memories mixed and blended into the others like the waters of an estuary. She became a network of memories as well as a network of matter.

Alva had arrived.

She knew this place, this sacred, beautiful place right beneath her hands and feet, held the secret to life in a new way. It could reignite her research profoundly. But, there was so much more. It meant the difference between life and death for her. A warm sensation of affirmation spread through her. The cure for her disease, the very thing that took her own mother away and slapped a ticking clock on her life, was just beneath her fingertips.

But this place. Unique in all the worlds. She knew, with the same certainty that had led her here, that if she took even a part of this being's body back, if she discovered a new medicinal breakthrough, if she published exciting cutting-edge research, this place would suffer. Researchers would swarm here. Companies would dispatch harvester drones. The primordial being of Oberran would die, and this place would be destroyed.

Alva drew her hand away. A kaleidoscope of light flooded her eyes as she shuffled backwards and gazed up at writhing limbs of the being's central core. They were still connected, the tiny human and this colossal intelligence. Even in death, Alva understood that she'd be part of something greater. The very fear that had driven her here— drove her to push her loved ones away—was now a sort of comfort. She had been staring down death for so long, she had forgotten what it truly was. There was no end. Not even in death. The being had collected her memories so she would live on for centuries, perhaps millenia, in the heart of Oberran. She would live on in the memories of her loved ones. Though she hadn't admitted it to herself, Alva had come to this place to die. Instead she had received a gift.

"Thank you," Alva whispered to the being. "Thank you for making me understand."

And the being replied in a thousand, thousand whispers. She looked up as an orb of green light descended towards her. It wasn't a spore cluster. It was a seed. It wasn't what she came for. It was what she needed. She reached above her head, and the seed gently landed in her hand, light and fluffy as down.

She closed her eyes, breathing in the thick air of the moon, breathing in the glowing lights of the being of Oberran, and Alva Asteris wept.

Andrew G. Cooper is an award-winning author, playwright, and screenwriter based in Calgary, AB. They are a member of the Playwrights Guild of Canada and a recipient of the Kamloops Mayor's Emerging Artist of the Year Award. They're also a puppeteer on Jim Henson's *Fraggle Rock: Back to the Rock*!

BAGEL THE BEAGLE

Lee F. Patrick

Calitha Akkadian-Truthell stopped in the station corridor as the alert tone chimed. She'd just finished her training shift in Enviro and was heading home. Her companion, her Robopet Bagel, stopped a few steps in front of her, then perked his ears as he sat and looked up at her. He'd been a present for her twelfth birthday from her oldest brother. Two years ago now.

"To all residents and visitors, anyone having knowledge of the current whereabouts of Jorny Somens are urged to contact Station Security. He is four years old, currently wearing a tan outfit. Light brown hair and blue eyes. Under a metre in height. Last seen at the play area on Beta Deck at 15:37. Please report any sightings after that time chop. Otherwise, keep to your duties and routines."

Silence. Calitha felt a moment of panic. Taking a deep breath, she looked down at Bagel. He had the form and behaviours of an Earth beagle, but with his AI, was potentially much smarter than any organic dog could ever be.

"I wonder if he just wandered off again," she said to Bagel. Jorny had done that before. A lot. He'd never gone very far before, and previously there hadn't been any announcements. She and Bagel found him four times before this. Mostly in the Beta Deck play area or heading toward it when he escaped from his mother.

"Wait, didn't his mum put a chip into him?" Bagel yipped once, then whinged with sad eyes and drooping ears. The feeling of dread was back.

"We'll go by their quarters and ask if we can help find him. Okay?" Bagel bounced to his feet and wagged his tail. Calitha sped up, not quite running toward the quarters Jony and his mom lived in.

Seven people waited quietly outside the door, including a security guard, to ensure no one entered the quarters. She ignored the neighbours and went up to the guard.

"Have you gotten any results from Jorny's tracking chip?"

The guard stared at her. "Wait one."

She tried not to fidget as the guard turned away and muttered into his comm. He shook his head. "No response from the chip, but those don't have much power. They've been pinging it every ten minutes. Boy must have gotten down into the ducts this time. Lousy contact with so many power conduits to overwhelm the signal."

"Bagel knows him. Maybe he can find him. We've done it before."

The guard looked down at Bagel, who sat down and wagged his tail.

"He's a Robopet," she explained, "based on a hunting dog. I'm studying Enviro and he can find all sorts of scents. We've also upgraded his sensors. Twice now."

"She's right," a voice said from behind her. "I've worked with Bagel in Enviro and he's good. Can't hurt since the boy's not showing up on the cameras." Specialist Warne Truthell-Synoms smiled down at Calthia and Bagel. Bagel wagged his tail at the Specialist in greeting.

Others in the crowd agreed. The guard turned away again, muttering into his comm. Calthia needed more deep breaths to keep from bouncing in place. Jorny could get into the really small spaces that adults couldn't. Bagel was a little over knee high on her. Forty centimetres at the shoulder. And he could crawl. He was small enough to follow Jorny just about anywhere. Eventually the guard turned back to them.

"Chief's heard about your pet before this, miss."

The apartment door opened and another guard handed out a set of sleepwear with multicoloured animals on it to the one outside. Then the door closed.

"These gotta be good enough to remind him of the boy's scent," the guard said. "I'm to take you to the point last seen. Specialist, why don't you come with us? The rest of you, head back to your quarters or duty stations. You can't help find the boy just standing here."

The guard started down the hall and Bagel trotted by her side just behind him. Specialist Warne walked beside her. "I'm Narten Synoms-Laidar. Just call me Narten."

"Have a lot of other people been in the playground since then?" she asked.

"Probably," Specialist Warne said with a sigh. "It's normal. People rush around to look where a dozen more just checked when someone's missing." He glanced down at Bagel. "Glad we did that sensor upgrade last week." They'd doubled the receptors on Bagel's tongue. Some were for taste but others were for odours, which had seemed odd to her, but maybe they'd run out of nasal passage surface area.

"I am too." Calthia took a deep breath. She wanted to

run to the play area but neither man broke out of a brisk walk. The only real sound was from Bagel's toenails clicking on the floor.

The play area was deserted when they arrived. It seemed cold in there, though she knew the temperature of the entire station was automatically regulated. They stopped just inside the main door. Bagel sat, looking at the sleepwear. Calthia held out her hand and Narten surrendered the cloth to her. She knelt next to Bagel and held it near Bagel's nose. "Bagel, find Jorny."

Bagel stuck his nose into the cloth in several places, then looked up at her, wagging his tail twice. His ears perked up.

"He's ready," Calthia told Narten, who shrugged. "Find Jorny. Stay close to me unless there's danger to Jorny or any other child. Defend."

A bark, then he trotted into the playground, staying near the outer edge of the room, nose checking all around.

"He's searching for the exit Jorny used," Specialist Warne said while they watched. "Calthia's also been teaching him about Search and Rescue procedures. Being small makes it easier for him to get into tight places."

"I'd just thought of him as a portable enviro sensor suite at first," Calthia said. "But he's very adaptable, we've found."

Bagel stopped in front of a closed storage room with a large grate above the doorway and barked twice before continuing on.

"Jorny was in there," Calthia said. "Wouldn't someone have checked inside it?" The searchers couldn't have missed him there, could they? It was one of the places they'd found him before. Her fists clenched with the effort of not shouting or running behind Bagel.

"They should have," Narten said. "We found another missing kid still in their bed a year or so back. They were between the bed and the wall, so the parents thought they'd run away. Kid even slept through us searching through the quarters. The kid was all confused when they woke up in a room full of people, getting a rib-cracking hug from their mom."

Bagel finished his circuit then trotted back to stand in front of the storage room. "Jorny must be in there," Specialist Warne said. "Don't know how anyone could have missed him."

Narten checked the control and opened the door then ensured it wouldn't close on them. Bagel glanced at her and she nodded for him to continue. He walked in but stayed in the middle of the path through shelves and containers of equipment. That meant the scent wasn't from Jorny trying to play hide and seek this time. Bagel stopped at a large mesh-covered vent in the back wall. This was a major ventilation trunk, she realised, large enough to walk in.

"That's strange." Narten said. "He couldn't have gotten out of here this way. Vent's still sealed."

"Bagel, was Jorny alone in here?" She clenched her fists. He wouldn't have the knowledge or the tools needed to open the vent cover. There had to be…

Two quick barks. Calthia swallowed before she spoke. "That means no."

"How many scents are here?" Narten asked.

Three barks. Then Bagel sniffed at the vent's surface. Two barks. Nose down, he headed back out of the storage area, stopping at the main entrance. Another bark.

"So one person stayed here and resealed the vent once they went in. I'm reporting in. Don't touch anything until I tell you."

Narten went out into the play area and Bagel came back to sit by her side. She patted his head. Specialist Warne looked at her. He was worried. For Jorny, even though she didn't think they'd ever met. But she'd mentioned looking for him before.

"Why would two men want Jorny?" she asked. She didn't really want an answer. Too many possibilities were flashing through her mind.

"We'll have to wait until we find them to ask them that question."

A growl came from Bagel.

She agreed with him.

"The station is being sealed," came the voice over the speaker system. "Please remain in your quarters or duty stations. If you are not on duty, please return to your quarters. All transient quarters are on lock-down and will be checked. All security go to level four."

Narten returned. "Unseal it."

Specialist Warne pulled out his belt's toolkit and knelt beside the vent. Calthia had never seen him without it, even in the mess hall.

Narten turned to Calthia. "We have new orders. Have you ever tried to see and hear what Bagel does in your SAR practice? In case the trail gets too narrow for us to follow him. Lights are on the way, but we still need to track him in there so security knows where we are."

"We've never tried that sort of link," she said. "Just a download of the compounds he identifies for various Enviro tests. But we might be able to stream his visual and auditory systems."

She pulled out her small comp pad. Narten handed her

a larger unit from his belt.

"This one is more powerful and I can easily re-route the feed to the Security office."

"We?" she asked. "You don't want to take just Bagel?"

"Both of us. You know how to interpret his reactions and what he can do. So you're coming."

Relief flooded through her. This was much better than being left behind. Plus, if Jorny was scared, he'd be more willing to come to her or Bagel than to a person he didn't know.

"We're going to follow him and whoever's with him. Specialist Warne, stand by here if we need to come back this way. Others will follow our progress to open any other vent we need to."

"Once we find him." Calthia said. Her voice was thankfully steady, not squeaky.

Calthia held the unit in front of Bagel. "Bagel. Access link to this unit. Allow streaming of all visual and auditory sensors to this and other locations. Implement." Mentally she crossed her fingers. She knew that Bagel's AI was good, but was it capable of this?

"He can access other computers?"

"Well, just sending data. But I think that module is from the sensor upgrades we did, not from anything already installed. We didn't have a full manual at first."

The screen flickered and suddenly showed Calthia's face. A happy bark, echoed a second later from the comp.

"Good boy!" Bagel wagged his tail so hard his entire body wriggled.

A thud and the vent cover hit the deck. Specialist Warne stuck his head in. "Walking passage. The airflow may make it harder for Bagel to follow them, but his sniffers can detect micro quantities of any chemical we've tried so far."

Narten took the comp. "Chief, are you reading the feed?"

"We are. I have a team reviewing the corridor camera feeds to identify and track the person who re-sealed that vent. Hoping to get a picture of the other one going into the play area."

A guard ran in with several headsets with attached lights. She and Narten put them on, but it took a moment to adjust hers properly since her head was still smaller than an adult's.

"Heading in now, sir."

"I'm not happy with the girl going in with you," the Chief said. "Calthia, stay behind your escort. Do *not* leave him to follow the dog unless he or I order you to. Do you understand?"

"Yes, Chief."

"Good. Head out, Narten."

"Heading out, sir."

Bagel went to the vent, sniffed, entered and turned right. Narten followed and Calthia went in behind him, still holding the comp. Now that she had purpose, she was calm. At least for now.

They stayed on the Beta level for two turns, then looked down a bare tube nearly a metre wide. Bagel looked over at her. Narten sighed.

"Okay. Chief, looks like we're heading down to Gamma level. I can chimney down with Calthia above me. Not sure on getting Bagel down." The only light was from their headsets and she tried to be careful not to look Narten directly. She'd been confused at the silence at first, then realised that Bagel had retracted his toenails so no one could hear them coming. She missed the tic-tic-tic noise he usually made as they walked along.

"He has a leash," Calthia said. "It comes out of the collar unit. We could tie it to your belt if we have to. I've had some climbing lessons. And the tube doesn't look very long." She looked at the map on the pad. "Just one level, according to the map. Four or five metres, I guess."

Bagel barked softly, then inched into the opening and

slid from sight. A happy bark a few moments later and they saw him in their headlights, wagging his tail as he looked up at them.

"You slide down first," Narten said. "Hold your feet together."

Moments later she was down safely. "All clear!"

Narten joined her moments later. "Bracing. Where's Bagel?" A bark further down a branch answered that question. "Let's catch up with him."

"I bet whoever this guy is, he doesn't know the system very well," Narten said after the third time they'd had to backtrack. "He must not have a full map of the vent system."

"Like we do," Calthia said.

They'd find Jorny before anything bad happened. They had to.

Nearly an hour and three tubes later, Bagel stopped near a waist high vent, its cover open. A faint male voice came from the other side. Narten took the comp and typed in a message. Moments later he nodded and slid the vent cover far enough over for Bagel to get through.

"Show us what's happening over there," he said softly. Bagel wagged his tail once and headed into the darkness.

Narten moved to sit against the side of the vent and

patted the deck on his right side, the one away from the opening, to indicate that she should join him. The comp's screen was completely dark, but he changed a setting and it changed to night vision.

"Doggie night sight," he said quietly. "Very handy. Don't whisper if you speak. It carries more than like this."

She nodded.

"You idiot," said a man not in view. "The alert went out way before it should have. What did you do once you left the playground?"

"Nothing! I sealed the vent after you left and went back to the air cleaner I'd been working on. People saw me working. Got off shift and came down here to seal this vent. Thought you'd be all done and gone by now. Wanted it all finished before anyone came in here to move the cargo."

A pause.

"Is the kid okay?"

"Drugged him first thing. Much easier than dragging a screaming kid through the vent system."

Another pause.

"The main reason I'm running behind is because the plans you gave me didn't show all the passages. I had to turn back five times. Any idea what set off the alarms?"

"Dunno. Maybe his mom went to pick him up early.

Let's get him in the crate so we can both get out of here."

The view changed to a thermal image as Bagel inched closer. Two tall shapes standing and one small one lying on the deck.

"Narten," the chief said into the headphones. "They're in an outgoing shipment hold. Twenty three J. Two security teams are inbound. Ensure neither man leaves that room before they're in place."

Narten typed a message rather than speak. '*Will stand by here. We're in the vent. Bagel has suspects and boy in view. Jorny's unconscious, they said. Thermal shows he's nice and warm.*'

"We still have Bagel's feed," the chief said.

"We should just leave him," said the second man. "Gotta bad feeling about this."

"This is the job," replied the first. "My orders are to remove the kid and terminate any witnesses. That includes you. If you'd done your job right, everything would be sealed up and I'd be on my way within a few hours."

The images changed. One man drew away from the other, arms up. "Okay. Let's get this done. We can get out through the vents. I loosened up a couple of other panels that lead into other storage bays last shift. Don't want to show our faces in this section if security are roaming around."

"You might have a plan," the first man said. Part of him vanished as he moved behind a crate and opened the lid. "But mine is a different one. This crate is big enough for me and the kid. Once he's inside and hooked up to the air system, you can leave. I'll just head out with him for my reward. You'll find your share in that account I had you set up."

"Fine." a surly tone. "Let's move him in."

Calthia watched as the small shape on the floor rose and was placed in the crate. The second man moved behind another crate after that. The first one moved suddenly and the second fell. Only a soft sound like a muffled cough came through the audio channel.

"Gun, maybe," Narten said. "Chief? We have a major problem."

"Take him down. Stun only, so we can get answers from him. That crewman might still be alive and he can give us other answers."

Narten handed her the comp and stood up moving quietly out into the storage bay. That nasty feeling returned.

"Bagel, help Narten. Protect Jorny." Calthia said. The picture wavered slightly as Bagel wagged his tail to show his acknowledgement.

There was more light and the screen went back to a normal view. A man stood over a crate, arms inside it.

Activating the life support module. Bagel moved closer. His head was low to the floor.

The man turned slightly to reach for something. He looked directly at Bagel.

"What in the Deep!"

Then Calthia saw the weapon. Aimed at Bagel. It looked huge. Bagel growled and leapt forward, the weapon filling the screen. Then it went dark. Another noise, like when the crewman had fallen.

A thud and clatter from a crate lid falling. Another growl followed by a hoarse scream. Sounds she couldn't identify. Bumps. More growls from Bagel. A buzz from a stunner. And a second. Then silence.

Calthia looked out, seeing a head high light bobbing toward a worklight. She knew she didn't have any of the right training for this but it was hard not to run out to find Bagel. Was he all right? She couldn't hear anything. She stayed low, in case she needed to hit the kidnapper below the knees with the comp pad if he came in after her, or was carrying Jorny.

"Clear!" Narten's voice came through the headset. She heard the sound of the large hatch opening. The one into the outer corridor, she guessed. "Calthia, I'm coming to you."

"All right." She crawled through the opening and turned on her light, aiming it at her feet so Narten could find her but not be blinded.

"Is Jorny all right?" she asked as Narten came up to her. "And Bagel?"

"They're both fine. Jorny slept through the whole ordeal. I'm going to lead you so you don't see the scene. Okay?"

"Did Bagel do anything bad?"

"He protected the boy. Shut your light off, and close your eyes." Calthia took a deep breath and did so. A second pair of hands took her other side after a little while.

"We're outside the storage bay," the stranger said. "Open your eyes now."

She blinked in the light. Lots of security guards and medtecs were in the corridor. So was her dad.

"Hi, honey," he said, his smile forced. "I'm going to take you back to our quarters right now. Bagel needs to be cleaned up and then we'll bring him home."

"Did he kill that man?"

Several people stared at her. "No, Bagel just grabbed his arm so he couldn't use the weapon. There was some blood from the crewman and Bagel got dirty before Narten could stun the kidnapper."

A bustle as Narten carried Jorny out to a waiting gurney and the attendant medical team. Two other gurneys waited down the corridor.

"That's right," he said, putting the boy gently down and standing back so the medics could do their work. "A quick rinse and he'll be good as new. I promise."

Calthia paced the length of the living room. Mom was busy making supper and Dad had gone to supervise Bagel's cleaning. How long did it take to wash off a little blood? Or had there been a lot of it? She wasn't sure she could eat. The smells were making her stomach upset.

The door finally opened and Bagel, head held high, trotted through followed by Dad. He raced over to her and leapt up into her arms. She sank to the floor, hugging him.

"You silly dog, you could have been hurt attacking that man!" Bagel's reply was to lick her face. Everything was back to normal now. "But I'm so proud of you!" A happy bark and more face licks ensued.

Lee F. Patrick is a Calgary author writing mostly SF and Fantasy. Lee has published five novels in three different series (Coalition of Shifters, Mind Games, and Assassins Justice) along with various short stories and Celtic style poems. You can find Lee on Facebook as @LeeFPatrick.

ACROSS THE DARK VOID

KT Wagner

The spiders have multiplied. The constant tinny hum of the spaceship masks their noises, but they're there, lurking at the edges of my vision. I turn my head and they disappear into crannies.

Eradication is no longer a possibility, if it ever was. There are too many.

Over the weeks I've generated plausible excuses for my lack of action: *The loneliness stayed my hand. I had a concern I might compromise the scientific equipment.* Just yesterday I typed *The cosmic web mesmerized me* into the log

All correct but none reflect the truth. Ground Control is not trustworthy.

I don't mention the distention of my cheek or the swelling that's closed one of my eyes or the heaviness in my limbs despite zero gravity. Maybe that's why I finally switched off the internal monitoring cameras. The second week out, I coated the camera lenses with a dry lubricant, but a crawling unease whispered I may not have found them all.

The engineers didn't provide much room for a human crew when determining the cargo capacity of the space shuttle. The ideal pilot had to be under 65 kilos, and 'relatively healthy'. The latter qualification meant free-of-plague-antibodies and it reduced the available pool to less than a dozen. All of us women. Conveniently, that suited the needs of the colony. They rounded us up and placed us in isolation. *Never too many baby-breeders*. My words, not theirs.

I didn't protest. On Earth, exposure to the plague is only a matter of time. Perhaps I could scrape together the cash to pay for drugs to slow the progression, but it only delays the inevitable. The shuffling, mindless, late stages of the disease don't bear thinking about. Nobody says it out loud, but the colony looks like the last hope for humanity.

I wasn't Ground Control's first or second choice. Maybe not even their third, fourth or fifth choice given the shortness of my remaining reproductive years. However, in the final stages of launch preparation, one of the loading crew bit the pilot's arm. By the time the security detail reached them, he'd gnawed through to the bone. They sent someone to retrieve their second-choice pilot from her cell and found her dead. Apparent heart attack. I now think the spiders had something to do with it.

Ground Control had released many of us the evening before. They found me as I trudged along the railway tracks, heading to check out a rental at a nearby trailer park. The previous night there'd been another meteor shower and I'd lain in a field to watch it. It tired me out and I curled up amongst the corn stalks and slept there. Odd. I never used to sleep very well.

This journey is one way. At first, I dreamed about those I left behind. Now, I barely remember their names.

In the event of my death, the sleeping pod is designed to preserve my organic matter. Ground Control didn't tell me this. I think the spiders must have. I trust them. I avoid the pod.

For the first two weeks of the journey, I slept in the pilot's seat. When I noticed a funnel web deep between a container labelled *mycorrhizae* and another labelled *cyanobacteria*, I took to securing my sleeping bag to the shuttle window.

The lights automatically dim every night cycle. I lay my face against the quartz glass, gaze into the expanse and wait on dreams. The smooth surface cools the heat in my cheek.

Contrived reality, a dry rustle of a voice in my head. It cackles.

The line between awake and asleep is no longer a certainty. The monitors might tell me, but I've stopped looking at them. The warning lights irritate me. I break a couple and an alarm goes off. My head pounds. Hours later the shrieking finally stops.

This might be the last supply run Earth manages. The plague spread faster than predicted and a cure is elusive. A group of scientists blamed the first meteor shower, but no one believed them. If they weren't all dead, they'd probably be saying, "We told you so."

A team of government scientists claim this ship's cargo will help address the terraforming issues the colony struggles with. The technicians sounded nervous as they explained this to me. Or maybe the microphones on their hazmat suits distorted their voices.

All around me are bio-containers of fungus, microbes, plants and insects. The spiders are particularly happy to be aboard.

I'm not a biologist or even a scientist, just an ordinary pilot. My job was to manually steer the shuttle past the dark side of Mars. I fulfilled my duty. Now I'm mostly excess cargo. If I survive the rest of the journey—eight long months—my genetics could further diversify the colony, but I'm not interested in bearing children.

I don't think the colonists will be either.

A jab of panic accompanies this random thought— more and more are intruding—and I stretch my arms in an attempt to dissipate my anxiety. Space sick, nothing more. It will pass.

Orb webs edge the rim of the window, cloak the control panel, and mute the annoying auto-pilot lights. Funnel webs bridge gaps between containers. The webs glow a faint, iridescent purple. Or maybe the swelling around my eye is affecting my vision.

I've still not seen a spider, but their webs are everywhere. They're here and waiting.

The spun fabric of the universe unfolds around the ship. The blacks and pale beiges of the early weeks have evolved into kaleidoscopes of swirling colour.

Reedy, garbled voices twist through static bursts from the radio. Ground Control continues to issue their shrill petty orders. It wasn't difficult to rotate the receivers slightly away from both Earth and the colony. The shift could be explained by the buffeting of space wind. Important, because Ground Control still has access to life support and other essential systems. Caution is best, for now. The spiders are working on a solution to silence Earth.

I pace around the pilot's chair, a kind of bouncy lurch that gives me something to do and perhaps staves off bone-density loss.

My fingertips brush a web. The strands are sticky and soft and not unpleasant. I run my hand through the silk and gather it onto my fingers.

Long ago, I lay next to grandmother and looked up while she spun fibre. I hold my hand out like a drop spindle, though I don't trust the memory. It feels new.

I rub the web-silk between my fingers, and the oils from my skin smooth and shape it into a narrow roll. My rhythm improves the less I concentrate. I spin a fine lavender-blue filament. Grandmother would be proud, except I'm pretty sure my grandmothers both died before I was born.

I gather more silk. Hours, perhaps days, float past. Calm replaces anxiety. Acceptance replaces calm.

Throbbing in my cheek brings me back to myself.

I hang centre-ship, facing the window and the galaxy. Earth is no longer visible, but one planet is less than insignificant among centillion's of celestial bodies. A speck on a mote of dust.

The web is complete. A spun dreamcatcher. It connects everything in the ship to me, and through me, them. I wriggle and the movement shivers out along the strands.

My cheek burns and prickles. Seeking relief, I rub it against the web. A crawling sensation spreads across my face. I close my eyes. The pressure in my cheek lessens.

The receiver spits out an angry burst. I open my eyes. A

few spider babies still scurry through the web, but most have settled in.

The shuttle continues on its journey to the colony. Our new home.

Surrounded by gnomes, gargoyles and poisonous plants, **KT Wagner** writes speculative fiction in the garden of her home on the west coast of Canada. She enjoys day-dreaming and is a collector of strange plants, weird trivia and obscure tomes. KT's short stories are published in magazines and anthologies. www.northernlightsgothic.com and @KT_Wagner

THE SIGNAL

Halli Reid

"Approaching quadrant O-Niner-Juliet, Captain." I called as I pulled the ship out of light speed, careful to keep us out of range of ARP 151: the black hole.

"Thank you Sammy," she said and turned to the navigation window.

The Mother Solar System was still a tiny spec on the screen, but its predicament was apparent with ARP 151 slowly approaching. We had arrived just in time.

"Gladys, can you make contact with the Mother Solar System yet?"

"No Ma'am," Gladys called from her console beside me. "Nothing gets through and nothing is received except the original distress signal." She fed the tapping pattern through the overhead speakers so we could all hear it yet again. When she placed certain filters on it the garbled static died down, morphing into a woman's voice speaking an unknown language. The signal was a quasi-stellar radio source Gladys was tracking as a pet project until the translation proved the message was urgent.

What is this I feel inside me?
Knocking hard against my bones?
How should such a thing betide me?
They were kids and now they're stones.

We were a cargo ship. We usually transported data or scientific instruments from one planet to another. A broad band electronic signal usually sufficed but some things, physical things, needed to be examined in person; meteorites, fossils, even living organisms if they could survive. For example, Balmor, the planet covered in worms, had an outpost station where scientists continuously shipped live specimens to interplanetary universities for study and dissection. This type of workload exploited society's insatiable need for information and made us wealthy.

When we first received the signal we were prepped for a mission of exploration- to make contact with another life form--but further bits of the message revealed this would be a rescue mission.

Dr. Gripend, the socio-linguist we were transporting from Balmor, explained how alien cultures sometimes used encrypted messages to bypass higher authorities.

"If a society found themselves under a sort of duress, they might rely on a form of encryption to convey an undetectable message. They might even lie about the truth. To use archaic terminology, the message would appear as fiction in order to deceive their oppressors. Their core cultural systems of metaphors are vastly foreign from our own, but I can make an educated guess." Gripend straightened his uniform. "The stones represent a foreign body of planets." He seemed confident in his assessment. "The knocking against bones means something has fallen out of orbit. The kids turning to stones means that all life will be wiped out. The message is definitely a grim distress call."

Captain Hartley pressed her fingers together. "This is your professional analysis?"

Gripend nodded. "I warn you, there is no way to date a radio signal. This message might have been bouncing around in space for hundreds of years. It could be so outdated the inhabitants have already perished."

Not wanting to give up hope, we worked non-stop to decipher more of the code. Gladys ran it through every simulation we had, bounced it off of every ion and gamma filter to clean up the noise. We hired the galaxy's best translators to figure out more of what the mystery woman was saying. After months of trials and tests we uncovered another small phrase.

No sooner had she made one snip and then another,

And six little kids all jumped out alive and well,

For in his greediness the rogue had swallowed them whole.

The translation told us these life-forms did not recognize the deadly threat they faced or they were helpless to do anything about it. The astrophysicist from Central Command explained how six planets could not survive being spat out of a vortex.

"There are such anomalies in the universe it is nearly impossible to comprehend all of its facets and abilities." He said. "Which is to say the "rogue" is the black hole in quadrant O-Niner-Juliet. Our instruments indicate a solar system is there on the brink of being sucked in. Central Command requests that you make this your mandate."

Captain Hartly squared her shoulders. "Sammy, change course to quadrant O-Niner-Juliet and let's see if we can make it there in time."

"Yes. Ma'am." I said. Dialing in the coordinates transformed us from cargo ship to rescue mission.

Even with every possible advance to light speed it would take four days to get there. Other obstacles were likely to slow us down; asteroids, bio-cosmic plants or animals, not to mention other ships crossing our path. The vastness of space can be a crowded place.

During our journey we solved the next piece of the message:

> *He came to the brook and stooped to drink*
> *But the heavy stones weighed him down*
> *So he fell into the water and was drowned.*
> *"The wolf is dead!" the kids cheered and they danced*
> *With their mother all about the place.*

We hired a cosmo-weapons expert to tell us what it would take to destroy a black hole. So I was forced to work with Doctor Jack Wontoo again; or at least the holographic image of him.

"This message. Could there possibly be another meaning?" he asked. "Destroying a black hole will cost…"

We stood around his hologram trying to bring him up to speed. His black eyes glanced my way a little too often. Of course, he recognized me. I'd left an unforgettable impression on him.

"We've consulted many experts who assured us the signal is a genuine distress call," Captain Hartley interrupted. "Our translation is as close to the original as possible."

"So, if the wolf is the black hole, the mother is the home star, then the heavy stones are the weapon used to destroy …"

"Yes. We've determined that." She interrupted again.

Dr. Wontoo tapped his holographic finger against his jaw. "Heavy stones… hmm… heavy stones. A black hole is already heavier than any stone. I think you've misread this. It's not the stones we need. It's the river. The black hole must fall into the river and drown. But how does one drown a black hole?"

He said he would get back to us. His doubts bothered me. Everyone here knew what they were doing and he didn't need to question our team. Not when his indiscretion lost me my post at Central Command and lead to this isolated assignment.

Reaching the Juliet quadrant gave a spectacular view. Millions of lights and meteors churned around the dark center of the vortex like liquid being sucked down a drain.

We couldn't get any closer without risking being drawn in. Gladys continued her attempt to reach someone on the com link but her efforts were futile.

Finally, Dr. Wontoo came up with an answer. "Antimatter." His hologram waivered in the artificial light. "You can convert your primary core into an antimatter chamber and release it into the vortex. The reaction could be minimalized with the proper equations but it is likely the ship will be destroyed."

Hartly brushed her fingers over the luminescent console, squared her jaw and said, "So be it."

The strategy team worked day and night answering to Doctor Wontoo's instructions. Frustration seeped from the skin of anyone working on the primary core. At one point I was struggling with a stripping tool and it slipped and sliced into my thumb.

"Damn it Jack, this isn't working." I punched the hologram like I had many times that week, knowing I would never make physical contact with his face, but it made me feel better.

"Sammy, calm down and let me help you. Pull the cable towards you." He said.

"I am pulling it." I yelled.

He sighed. "Your behavior will embarrass you when you see me in person."

"What? You're coming here?" The pliers slipped from my grip and clanked on the floor.

"Our rescue convoy embarked this morning."

Pulling off my gloves, I wiped my brow leaving a smear of sweat on my sleeve. "I'm taking a break," I said.

"Sammy, we don't have time to…"

"I said, I'm taking a break." I left the hologram in the primary core to bother someone else.

We had four days to build the chamber, release it, detonate it, and get out of there. After that, the Mother Solar System would enter the point of no return. The grab zone. The end of chances.

"I'm reading life signs on two of the orbiting planets but I can't tell what species or level of intelligence. For all we know we could be saving a planet covered in worms like Balmor." I complained to Gladys. I knew she didn't want to hear it, this was her baby after all.

"Then they're worms that can speak and send signals into space." She put her headset on. For hours she sat at her station trying to send messages out to Mother Star in the off chance someone or something could pick it up but the black hole sucked in every frequency. Nothing new ever came back, only the loop of the distress call.

We got the anti-matter chamber finished hours before the rescue convoy came out of light speed. I wanted to tell Dr. Wontoo to turn right around because he was more useful as a hologram but I kept quiet.

The Captain addressed him with an unnecessary reverence. "Oh, thank you so much for coming and giving yourself for this mission. You are truly noble."

Since when did Hartly bow down to anyone? Especially some lowly cosmo-weapons specialist. I must have looked puzzled because Gladys whispered in my ear, "The detonation has to be done manually."

I looked at Gladys and Wontoo and Hartly, a light bulb snapping on in my head. "Show me," I whispered.

The plan was to evacuate the ship and let Dr. Wontoo steer her towards the center of the black hole. Right before it ripped the ship apart he would eject the core, then try to back out with only the central engines; meant for docking not battling a giant vacuum. The chamber would collapse exposing the anti-matter and if his math was right the vortex would merely evaporate. If his math was wrong he would blow up the universe. The giant vacuum should then release the Mother Solar System, the ship, and Jack, if he wasn't already dead. Communication lines would open and allow us to see exactly who it was we had saved.

"Ridiculous," I muttered.

When the last crew member was jettisoned to the convoy I made sure I wasn't with them. Captain Jack entered the upper deck and flipped when he saw me.

"What are you doing here? There are no pods left. Are you crazy?"

"No, but I am the pilot and I'm going to pilot this baby into a black hole while you release the chamber."

"You're an idiot, Sammy."

"No, you are, Jack. You never could have done both by yourself. So calm down and let me help you." I smirked at using his own words.

The ship rattled under growing pressure. I quickly took my seat at the helm checking instruments. "We are at 80% stability." The lights flickered. "You'd better get down there and release the chamber on my command.

"And how do you know when the timing is right?" he asked.

"Easy." I adjusted my uniform. "At the last possible moment." I made a shooing motion and he obeyed.

From the convoy, Hartley's voice came over the intercom. "Sammy, what the blazes do you think you're doing?"

"Being a pilot ma'am. Obviously Dr. Wontoo needed me."

"And after you implode? What then?"

"I'm redoing our navigation and if the convoy stays relatively close you will have time to collect us and still break free of the gravitational pull. Sending my calculations now." My hands swept over the console firing data at the rescue convoy.

Gladys came on. "Leave the signal playing in case you get close enough for anything new to come through."

"Ten-four." I opened the audio channel on the overhead speakers and fed it through her preprogrammed filters.

"We may lose contact …" The feed from the convoy cut out.

Out the navigation window I could see the other ship and willed it to maintain its position risking every life on board to give us a chance - a very slim chance of surviving.

"I've reached the primary core." Jack's voice buzzed through the speaker competing with the looped signal.

"Structural integrity at 50% and dropping fast." I told

him. "What are the chances you can make it to an escape pod once the chamber is released?"

He laughed, "Nil. They are all gone."

"Every last one of them?" I checked the status map. Every pod was lit up red. "Why?"

"Because we are not getting out of this."

"You shut up." I barked. "And put on a space suit. I have another idea."

"Yes ma'am." Was mixed in with:

For in his greediness the rogue had swallowed them whole.

The nasty rogue, he was going to swallow us whole. At least try to. I whipped on a space suit and checked the reading again. "Stability at 30%."

"Is it time?" He asked.

"Not yet."

The lights pulsed on and off. The floor and walls shook as if we were inside a furious hurricane. I turned the ship vertical so the chamber hatch was closest to the black hole.

"Reversing engines." I had to yell over the groaning of the hull. "We are slowing down."

"Sammy, we've got to release the chamber! The ship is breaking apart!" Jack's voice was frantic.

"Not yet!" I yelled. My heart dropped into my stomach.

In order to get the chamber into position it would have to get past the flare of the engines without breaking. I would have to turn them off, leaving us completely vulnerable to the giant vacuum outside.

My face flushed with heat. "Now!" I screamed into the mic and killed the engine.

The power went out. The coms went dead. The status map showed nothing.

I ran to the front window and pressed my helmet against the barrier, trying to see the tail end where the chamber should appear. Sparkling space-matter span around like a carousel but no chamber joined the race. I waited. I pounded my fist against the barrier. The ship tilted closer to the vortex.

"Come on!" I prayed, banging my helmet.

Then I saw it: a tiny grey box came around the side of the ship, swirling into the crowded accretion disk, jostling with asteroids and glowing space dust.

"Yes!" I leapt back to the helm, "Engines in full reverse!" I snapped the ignition on and pulled the accelerator back as far as it would go. Nothing happened. My eyes darted around for a solution but the console was dark. I slammed the lever back and forth. "Get working you piece of junk!" I kicked the console breaking one of my toes.

The coms buzzed on. "Calm down and let me help you." It was Jack. "I can reroute the power from here."

I think a tear fell down my cheek. Or it was sweat. The engines turned over. I jammed the helm to maximum thrust, knocking myself to the ground. The ship righted itself and I aimed her nose straight at the convoy in the distance.

"Jack, get out of there." I warned. "The mass of the hull will drag us in. Separate it from the deck."

"Yes ma'am." He replied.

The ship was shaking, but barely moving. We were trapped in the grab zone, past the point of no return. Without the primary core we didn't have enough strength to outrun the gravitational pull. Central Command would lose a transport ship and two crew members. I checked the sensors to find the anti-matter chamber speeding around the swirling accretion disk, still intact and containing the antimatter. The Mother Solar System was on the brink of falling out of alignment but still in the safe zone.

Then I remembered Gladys's link. I flipped the switch to transmit.

"Hello? Mother Solar System, does anyone hear me? Can you read me? Are you safe?" I called, running my voice through the filters and out as a series of beeps, matching the frequency of the distress call.

A message came back.

It wasn't what I expected at all.

"Is it true Mummy? Can you be swallowed whole by a wolf and still be alive?"

"No dear, this is just a bed-time story. It's not real. Now, time for bed."

The signal ended. I stared blankly at the speaker with my mouth open. A bed time story? What in the universe was a bed-time story? Why would anyone transmit an untrue message?

Something caught my eye. The direction of the signal had changed. Now that we were close enough I could see the origin of the message was not the Mother Solar system at all. The black hole had warped the path of the signal, bouncing it from who knows where and who knows how far away and for how long... The stupid signal could be thousands of years old. I broke another toe on the console.

Dr. Wontoo burst into the room. "Sammy!"

I limped towards him let him wrap his arms around me. For a brief, silent second our helmets touched. I sucked in a breath and led him out the door, my heart pounding. "Follow me."

I took him to the weapons launch bay, yelling over my shoulder. "The torpedoes are launched with pressurized air. It can eject us out of the grab zone and close enough to the convoy to be collected." I got to the nearest tube and flung open the breech door. "Get in."

"How sure are you this will work?" he asked.

I didn't answer and he didn't ask again. He clambered inside while I started the automated launch sequence.

As I was about to lock him in, Jack spoke. "Sammy," He called from inside the tube. In the darkened tunnel only his feet were visible. "Thanks for staying with me."

I paused, smiled, reached in to pat his boots then closed the breech door.

Special acknowledgement to the Brothers Grimm

Halli Reid (Lilburn) has stories published with Tesseracts, Renaissance Press, and many others. She is a freelance editor with Essential Edits and collaborated with Coffin Hop Press to edit *The Dame Was Trouble*. She has taught creative writing at Casa in Lethbridge as well as presented at When Words Collide and other conferences. She is a librarian, artist, mother, feminist and literary hoarder. She is ACE and ADHD and sometimes stares off into the void with profound purpose.

ALIEN LOVER

Nancy Kilpatrick

My lover is an alien. Not a person from another culture, but a being from another planet.

Many women feel that way about men, of course, and vice versa; it's a statement of how disparate the genders often seem to one another. But that's not what I'm talking about. I'm talking about a *real* alien. A being unlike any other that walks this planet.

I'm not a patient in a mental hospital, writing this on scraps of toilet paper, and I'm not some SoHo performance artist who wants to shock and enlighten. I'm just a woman, an ordinary human being. And because of destiny, I managed to hook up with Thomas, or at least that's the name I call him since the sounds he makes are enough like that name that I find it comfortingly familiar.

From the start, I'll admit that I've always had a fascination with extraterrestrial life. That may taint some of what I'm about to say. Even though the majority of North Americans, if not citizens of Earth, believe that intelligent life exists in space, admitting to that seems tantamount to implying eccentricity at best and lunacy at worst. I will also acknowledge that I went through a period of time—about a year actually—when my marriage was breaking down, when I'd drive around Philadelphia at night in my little silver Toyota searching the skies. Of course, as Fox Mulder would have been the first to tell us, a city is the last place where a spaceship would land. The fact that I, like most people, know that didn't stop me from looking. But then I was close to a breakdown. Whenever I traveled on business or for pleasure, I'd rent a car and drive around—in Atlanta, in Phoenix, in Stanford, Connecticut. I did not see any ships or any aliens. I was not a passenger on one of the commercial aircraft where the pilots saw alien vessels trailing their Boeings. I did not visit that town in the Yukon where the entire population saw lights that were not the aurora borealis streak across the sky for several nights in a row. I have never been aboard an alien craft, either voluntarily or as a kidnap victim, and have not been the subject of alien medical probes. At least not that I remember.

That year of searching the skies was an anomaly in my

life. And when the divorce was finalized and I began to heal emotionally, I read Carl Jung and something he said, about spaceships and extraterrestrial life being symbolic of a search for the divine and a latent desire for wholeness, well, that made sense to me.

Besides Jung, I read a lot of science fiction. From the novels and short stories, there seem to be several theories of why these beings come to Earth. Foremost is to make contact. Another reason is to keep tabs on us, the techno-idiots of the universe. To invade our planet and take it and its citizens for their own is a third, and to intermingle and create a new species is last, but not least. But I've discovered another reason they come here; at least with Thomas that seems to be so.

We met in Toronto. I was there on business, staying at one of the chain hotels on Lake Ontario where the computer conference was being held. It was summer, a pleasant evening, and I decided to take a walk along the harbor of this notoriously-safe city.

The sun had just set, but the sky was still light. Cars sped by on the above-ground roadway behind me, far enough in the distance to not be annoying. As I gazed out over the lake, boats with white sails dotted the water, and I watched ferry boats carrying people back and forth between the mainland and a five-mile strip of terra firma called Toronto Island. I walked slowly along the flag-stoned harbor path breathing deeply the fresh air and stopped to rest against the ropes that acted as a barrier between land and water.

We've all had that feeling, of someone staring at our back. In the twilight, I sensed him and turned to my right. Coming along the path was a man with white hair and who wore a white suit. He was not old, but in his late thirties, my age, or so it seemed to me then, although then as now I cannot clearly recall his face; he possesses a timeless quality. His body emitted some type of invisible energy that drew my attention. I know that sounds very New Agey, but believe me, other than that year of living dangerously close to the border of breaking apart, I normally have my feet firmly planted on the ground.

When he reached me he just stopped and turned, so that he, too, stood facing the water. It was as though we were old friends who didn't need words to communicate with one another. We simply stood there, inches apart, shoulders almost the same height.

Now, I do not normally talk with strangers, except in a crowded place, like a bank, a restaurant lineup, or at a business conference, and then it's cursory and polite, the conversation pointed. I'm not paranoid, simply cautious. Being in a strange city usually inspires extra caution. And since there were no other people along the waterfront, at any other time I would have walked away.

Why did I stay there? I've thought about that a lot.

There's the obvious—I was lonely. But loneliness has never been enough reason to cause my good sense to abandon me before, other than my search for spaceships, and I think I've explained that. With all the pondering I've done, though, I still can't honestly say what kept me there, other than that I felt something happening that I liked. It was as if the level of iron in my body had been seriously depleted and I hadn't been aware of it. Then, suddenly, my receptors were open and reaching out toward this being to be replenished. I know that sounds vampiric of me, and I suppose that our relationship is like that in a way. But there's more to this relationship. Much more.

But that first evening, we stood at the water's edge until the sky darkened and the new moon rose. I was keenly aware of him, the power of the energy that pulsated from him. That intensity left me afraid to actually look at him. But when I did turn, he turned also, mirroring me, as if he were a mime. I stared into pale almond eyes that seemed to darken and then lighten as I watched them. They enlarged and emitted a warmth that cocooned me from head to toe. Had he touched me physically the sensations could not have been stronger. I found myself gasping, overwhelmed by a kind of passion I had not envisioned existed. It was like orgasming on the sidewalk, and I was both afraid and excited.

Suddenly, he turned. Whatever energy connected us connected us still. As he walked away, I was pulled along behind him by invisible bonds.

We walked and walked, as far as the harbor path would take us, then through a park, then to a marina. At the far end he boarded what I can only describe as a black metallic vessel that blended with the night so well, it seemed to be invisible. I trailed behind him up the midnight gangplank, my heels clacking against the metal, still engulfed by silky yet invisible threads of passion kneading me. Once down below deck, he shut the door and we were plunged into complete darkness.

It was at this point that I became aware of being very afraid. I've never felt comfortable in the dark, and there I was, in a peculiar, isolated place, with a stranger, in a strange city. I tried to speak but found I couldn't form words. I imagine this is what aphasia feels like: you know the concept you are trying to get across, but can't quite remember how to say the words. Although I was not physically bound, I might as well have been, because I was unable to move.

My eyes became accustomed to the metallic blackness. I couldn't actually see anything identifiable, but I had vague impressions, one of which was this man—for a few moments more I still thought of him as just a man—standing there, facing me, silently. I realized my heart was beating hard, and my lungs were filling and expanding rapidly. Chilly sweat coated my body, and my limbs trembled.

I wanted to ask him what he was doing to me which left

me immobile. I wanted to know why he had brought me here and what he had planned. I wanted to know who, no, *what*—because by then I began to realize that he was not quite human. I wanted to ask him why he had no scent. Of all the other questions, that was the one that startled me most when I became aware of it. I simply could not smell him. Stainless steel has a smell. Even plastic has an odor. And certainly anything organic. But he did not. And although my own sense of smell has never been outstanding, it isn't bad and I recognized that scent was the one sense missing.

Finally, when I thought my heart might not be able to take the tension any longer, a sudden wave of calm rolled over me. I realized he was flowing closer—that I *could* sense.

Oddly enough, the closer he got—as he had at the harbor—the more my anxiety turned to pleasure, and the pleasure to passion. When he reached me physically, I gasped.

He lit up—that's the only way I can put it—phosphor in a metallic night sky. The light took the shape of his body, but more than his body, as if what the psychics call an 'aura' was visible and his solid molecules actually mingled with the air molecules and I could see no clear division between them. There were colors I recognized, but many I did not, as though he used a different spectrum and my eyes could finally see what they normally were unable to distinguish. Colors that had the intensity of red and yet were more like combinations of blackened silver and yellow and peach, although that does nothing to describe them or do them justice. I found the visuals fascinating. So much so that I did not at first realize that his body was enfolding mine. The colors that he vibrated encased me and then I felt them enter every pore in my flesh. But they entered me as a scent, like thousands of tiny vapors working their way into every pore. The scent was new to me, more pungent than sweet or tart, greater than anything I had encountered before. It was a penetration I could not have envisioned and one that kept me on the edge of something akin to climaxing in a delicious, delirious state of almost being sated. A state where time and space became meaningless and all that mattered was this essence that filled my body through my pores as, by way of a poor analogy, the smell of roses would have filled my nasal cavities and lifted my spirits. And through it all, I heard him. And yes, it is likely that in my fragile humanity I reached out and used the sounds to form a name, to find something familiar...

In the morning—and I must skip to daybreak because I cannot honestly remember details—I found myself lying on the path at the harbor where I'd first seen him. There was no sign of him. No sign that he had even been there. And, of course, my sanity returned. With it, anxiety surged. It wasn't long before I was at a police station, filing a complaint with them, trying to describe a man I could not remember visually with a crime that seemed like rape but which I could not articulate.

I scanned hundreds of photos. The dark metallic ship was gone, of course. The police dusted the harbor ropes for fingerprints and found only mine. And the worst part of it all was that a physical examination revealed no signs of intercourse. I couldn't bring myself to tell them that the entry had been through my pores as well as every orifice of my body, but I did ask for a skin analysis. Nothing unusual showed up. And by the time the DNA results of blood and vaginal secretions finally came through, I was back home. Only my own DNA was present.

That encounter occurred a year ago. I went through much trauma and soul-searching. I even saw a psychiatrist for a few sessions—until the next new moon.

Every month, at the first sliver of a moon, Thomas shows up, no matter where I am. I could be home alone in my living room. At a movie with friends. Working overtime. Traveling again. Each time it is the same. I am drawn to him as if my body needs to recharge. He takes me someplace where we can be alone. And I go willingly. And then he is recharging as well, with what he gets from me, through my pores, whatever that is. I still don't know.

I have been afraid. Utterly terrified to be precise. Never with him, but between the times when I see him. And what terrifies me most is how much I long for him.

It took me three months to realize it was the moon that

determined when he would appear, which leads me to feel that the moon plays on him as it plays on our tides. Perhaps his home is a moon, black and metallic. It took time to realize the symbolism of what the new moon represents. It took time for me to realize exactly how I have changed.

Needless to say, I am different. Whereas once I was outgoing, now I live only for those hours when I am with Thomas. I am obsessed. Yet to my family, friends, and colleagues I am the same woman I have always been. I go about my business and interact in familiar patterns. But my life is like an orange with the juice extracted from it. When we are together Thomas gives to me, but he also takes from me and in his wake leaves behind an ever-hollowing shell. Oddly enough, I do not hold this against him. Somehow, it makes me love him more.

Physically, I am constantly dehydrated. That, of course, leaves me exhausted, but then, as the new psychiatrist says, I'm depressed, but the anti-depressants do not help. I have many of the symptoms of HIV and yet the tests are negative and no virus can be isolated. The doctors are stymied by that, and more so by what they have labeled a noxious odor my body emits. The colors with their wondrous fragrance that Thomas leaves inside me seem to transform into something not so pleasant to others. To hear people talk, you would think I was rotting inside, and one day I will wake up and be nothing but decay. But the decay smells sweet to my nostrils because it reminds me of him.

And Thomas? Each time I see him I know he is stronger. His colors smell brighter and more vivid, and their range has expanded the spectrum of hues. He lives while I die. It seems unfair, and yet what he gives me is all that has meaning in my life. All that keeps me going. All that matters. And I would gladly give him every drop of my existence for one more breath of that alien scent.

It amazes me now that I spent an entire year searching the heavens for aliens when one was walking this planet. Is that why he found me, because I searched for him? What he shows me I realize is his home planet, which must be so far away, perhaps in another galaxy, or even another time or dimension. I do not know exactly why he has left there and come here, but I feel he is the only one of his kind and that he has found a way to survive. I feel, too, his loneliness. Except for me, he has no contact, although I could be wrong. It's possible that every night he absorbs the essence of another who acts like a battery providing him energy until the battery itself dies and is either recharged, or a replacement is found. But I don't think so. I think that it is *my* essence he wants and needs, and my greatest worry is what he will do when I'm gone. Because I know in my heart that he does not understand death. On his planet, wherever he comes from, life continues in black-star darkness, an ever-changing form. It is simply a matter of revitalizing. He cannot know that we poor mortals who strive for wholeness do so in order that we might blend with the whole, with the divine, with what is larger than us and we hope will absorb us when our frail bodies can no longer contain who we are.

What I have come to understand is that as he nourishes me, I nourish him, and it's possible that internally he is changing as I am. Why do I think that? Because I can now smell him. And he smells sweet. Very very sweet. The sweet essence of all life itself, the life of planet Earth. It makes sense to me; that's why he has come here. To take me in.

Award-winning author **Nancy Kilpatrick** is a genre writer and editor. Her twenty-three novels include her current series *Thrones of Blood*, recently optioned for film and television. She has published over 220 short stories, seven collections of her stories, one non-fiction book, and has edited fifteen anthologies.

THE SPACE BETWEEN US

Jarrod K Williams

Neil Finn propped his green Chuck Taylors on the console. He fiddled with his headset cord. The mission control room buzzed with activity, but no one would tell the funder to leave the room.

"Team is a go, Mission Control," Dr. Jane Sawyer said.

"Yeah, you are," Neil said.

"I thought you were at the shareholder meeting. Won't your dad be pissed?"

"And miss this? Forget it. They can email me the PowerPoint." His father could wait as Neil patted the small golden ring in his pocket. It once was his mother's, but he aimed to give it to Jane after she returned from the expedition. That was worth risking the fury of Finn Technical's CEO.

"Could the love birds get off the channel? We are starting the countdown," Dr. Dana Prewitt said. Jane's partner and best friend tolerated Neil on a good day, but today he intruded on her moment of triumph. Neil's humor masked his nerves. He wanted Jane to be safe, but Jane wouldn't let anyone else test out the interplanar bridge.

"Be safe," Neil said. He fought and failed to keep emotion from his voice.

"I will. I love you," Jane said.

"I love you too." Neil choked up.

Dana glared as she tapped on her watch.

"Mission control beginning countdown. Bridge will engage in 20," Dana said. Her voice echoed weirdly in Neil's head as he heard her both next to him and in his headset. Neil placed his feet on the ground and watched the large monitor screen as the countdown continued. A flurry of voices bounced around in his head as the energy actuators powered up in the room.

Streaks of bright yellow ran alongside the wall. They rotated, forming a tube completely of light where the sterile walls had been.

"10...9...8."

The crew on the monitor adjusted their equipment containing cases for samples and survival packs in case the worse happened and they were disconnected from Earth. Jane bounced back and forth from her left to right leg. She hated waiting in lines more than anything in the world. This line kept her from completing her life's work.

"7...6...5."

"Power levels stable. Tunnel structure secure. Opening portal now." Dana's status reports failed to comfort Neil. The tube rotated around the crew. The lines of yellow morphed into a spinning cylinder of light and hid the crew from view. The monitor switched to the camera mounted on Jane's suit.

"4...3...2...1." The end of the tunnel opened up onto a rocky terrain with a loud crack.

"Team deploying," Jane said.

The group advanced into the new world.

The mission control room erupted. Hugs and shouts of celebration surrounded Neil, but his focus was only on the monitor. This team turned the impossible into the possible and created a bridge to another world.

"Take care. You have sixty minutes before we close the tunnel." Dana flailed her arms for everyone to get back to work. She covered her microphone and whisper yelled, "There will be time for that when we get them back."

The planet seemed uninhabited, but there were fascinating readings coming off the rocks. The team packed several containers with them and ferried the cases back.

"Half the team is returning. Other half will follow," Jane said.

"Roger that," Dana said. The view on the monitor switched from Jane's camera to the group coming back. In the middle of a rocky wasteland stood a portal that showed their building and where the group had come from. The sight made Neil doubt his sobriety.

"Power levels are fluctuating. We have a problem." Someone called to Dana. She ran to their station. Neil watched the power levels coming into the building crater over her shoulder. The lights dimmed as they switched to emergency power.

"Jane, get out of there now. We're losing power." Dana's voice didn't betray any panic but it clawed up Neil's throat. He froze in place as the staff whirled around killing unnecessary functions.

"On our way." Jane's voice held steady. Neil gripped the arms of his chair.

"They will be fine," he repeated to himself like a mantra. "Get her back," Neil said to Dana. She glared at him.

"Keep the window open as long as possible." Dana commanded the room. Lights shut down and the monitor blinked out, but the portal held.

"Portal destabilizing," one of the workers on the portal floor said.

"It's falling too fast." Dana whispered to herself. "Take cover Jane. The portal is about to…" She was interrupted by a complete power failure. The portal winked out of existence, and they sat in blackness.

The love of Neil's life was stuck on the other side of the universe.

Neil and Dana sat in a dimly lit meeting room. Two laptops sat open in front of them. Papers covered the desk and white boards on each wall were covered in scrawled writing.

"So, it was a squirrel?" Neil asked.

"Officially it was a 'failed redundancy', but a squirrel chowed down on a transformer cable so it blew. Our generators had water mixed with the diesel, so they kicked on and quickly died."

"We open a portal to another world and are thwarted by a squirrel." Neil swore and slammed his hand on the desk. Dana sat back in her chair and appeared to be counting ceiling tiles. "We have to get her back. Any ETA on when the power grid will be restored?"

"You're not going to like this. It's going to be at least a month." Dana wouldn't meet his eyes and Neil's anger blazed.

"Really? How long does it take to replace a transformer?"

"It's a custom transformer in a remote location. They have to refabricate the parts. It's going to take a month just to assemble the new one, much less get a crew out here." Dana leaned forward and folded her hands together.

"Can the new generators power the machine?" Neil asked.

"No, it's not enough. They are emergency power only."

"Can we use the solar generators to bank power?" Neil grasped at straws, and he knew it.

"That's…" Dana paused as she cocked her head to the side, "…Not a bad idea. I don't know if it will work, but we can get right on it."

"What did we get out of this trip anyway?" Neil

searched for any positive of this mission.

Dana picked up a case off the ground and placed it on the table. "Several samples of this rocky mineral. We are analyzing what they are now, but it's too early for conclusions."

"I'll make a few calls to see if I can't speed up the power grid work."

"All units in position," Dana said. The radio communication answered with several folks in affirmative. "Power holding steady. Go or no go. It's your call Neil." The team had worked night and day for the past week to refill the power banks on the machine. The generators ran for days and the solar panels helped.

"Bring them home," Neil said.

"Affirmative. Begin ignition." The room on the monitor started to fill with yellow lights and they began to spin. The tunnel formed and spun. The team advanced as the machine whirred to life.

Neil sat on the edge of his seat. He fingered the golden ring in his pocket. This time he would bring her home. His heart leapt as the tunnel cracked and the portal opened. There were people on the other side. He saw Jane and his heart dragged him to his feet. The machine spluttered. The portal closed and the machine powered down. The yellow lights stopped and blinked out of existence.

"What happened?" Neil shouted.

"We didn't have enough juice." Dana's eyes watered and her voice choked.

"I'll be in my office. Come see me when you have the data." Neil fled to his office. Once the door was shut, he wept.

"What options do we have?" Neil asked. After a week of swearing and slammed doors, Dana sat in his office with a couple of other members of her team. They squeezed on the couch that sat alongside the back wall of his office. Neil had slept there many nights when Jane worked late. Neil hated being in these familiar places. Her presence lingered behind every corner.

"We tried the generators and solar cells and failed. We can't get up and running without attaching to the power grid. The only way that gets done faster is to get that transformer created from a private machinist. We need more money." Dana rolled her chair close to the desk. She hadn't wanted to squeeze into the couch, so she brought her own office chair.

The other scientists glared jealously.

"I'm tapped out. The trust won't front me any more money."

Dana's face flushed red as she snapped. "Then what do you want me to do, Neil? You wanted options. I gave them to you."

"Get out." Neil seethed. "Not you," he said Dana tried to follow the others as they got up and walked out. One of the scientists stayed behind.

"I should really brief you on this," she said with a file in her hand. Dana took the file and shooed her away.

"I'll inform him. You can go."

"OK." She stared at Dana before leaving and closing the door behind her.

"Dana, I already called my dad. He wouldn't spend any money on my passion project." Neil made air quotes over his last two words.

"Unless you have a carrot to dangle." She opened the file and placed it on his desk.

"What am I looking at here?" Neil read over the data on this graph. Something was producing an amazing amount of energy. Nothing they had discovered.

"The conductivity of this rock is off the charts. The top

graph is energy production from the current fusion reactors Finn Technical makes. The bottom graph is the simulated energy production based on the using the new mineral as the conductive material in reactor construction."

"This can't be right. Those rocks increase energy production exponentially." He stared at the graphs in disbelief and glanced back at Dana.

"It is a theoretical impossibility, but we have them in our lab."

"Something to change the game."

"Back of the napkin math says investment is ten percent more than a typical fusion reactor, but a thousand percent more energy."

"That's…" Neil trailed off.

"One hell of a carrot to dangle for your father."

"Dana, thank you."

"Don't screw this up. You get one shot."

"My dad's dream come true. Me begging for money hat in hand." Neil leaned back in his chair.

"What are you willing to do to get her back?" Dana gripped the door handle.

"Anything."

Neil sat in the chair outside his father's office. His knees bounced up and down as he rehearsed the pitch he and Prewitt had crafted. His normally unkempt hair was slicked back, and he traded his jeans and Chuck Taylors for a crisp grey suit and blue tie.

The receptionist typed away at the small white desk that stood outside the mahogany double doors that served as the gateway into the inner sanctum of Finn Technical, his father's corporate conglomerate kingdom. She apologized multiple times for his father's three-hour delay, but such was his way.

Sebastian Finn was relentless, and Neil remembered many times he missed a little league game or a school play because there was an issue at the office. Neil knew the delay was due to the problem of the day, but he also suspected this was a test.

Neil never kept his temper around his father.

The office doors swung open. The top two lawyers of Finn Technical exited. Uncle Bobby and Aunt Tamera were present throughout Neil's memories. The CFO and a couple of people exited behind him. They nodded politely at Neil, but didn't engage further. Sebastian Finn followed them out. His sharp grey eyes found Neil. He smiled, but it didn't reach those steely eyes.

"Cornelius, I apologize for the delay come on in." He shook his son's hand then placed one hand on Neil's back and gestured forward with the other. "I hope I haven't kept you from playing video games or whatever it is you do at Otherworld." Sebastian Finn delivered needles with the deft hand of an acupuncturist.

"It was no problem. Hopefully I'm not interrupting something important."

"Just a merger negotiation." They entered the cavernous room. It could have held three offices. There was a sitting area on the right-hand side of the room with a couch, a loveseat, and two wingback armchairs in matching neutral prints. On the left-hand side of the room was a drafting table and multiple whiteboards. In the center was the monstrous oaken desk with three small brown chairs in front of them. Sebastian took his seat behind the desk and gestured for Neil to take one of the chairs in front of the desk.

The backlighting made his father appear to have a halo. The bookshelves behind him held a mix of his degrees and framed magazine covers bearing Sebastian's picture. This was no mere office; this was a king's throne room.

"You know the board missed you the other day."

"I'm sorry."

"Your absence was conspicuous."

"I was at an important product test at Otherworld."

Sebastian nodded, but his eyes screamed he thought Neil was lying.

"You'll do well to make the next one, ok?"

"I'll try, Dad."

"That's all I ask," Sebastian said. "What did you want to talk to me about?" He refocused on the topic at hand.

"Otherworld needs help. Financial help."

"I see." Sebastian pressed his fingertips together and leaned back in his chair. "Why does your passion project need money?"

"The test we conducted the other day was both wildly successful and went completely wrong."

"Son, we've talked about this. I can't be bailing you out. No one saved me as I built the largest tech conglomerate in the United States."

Neil bit his lip before he said, "We created a bridge to another planet, but half our away team was stranded there. We need the funds to repair the machine to retrieve them."

"You did what?" Sebastian's disbelief dripped off every word.

"We were able to successfully contact another world. See our data." Neil reached into his black leather bag and placed a file folder on his father's desk. Sebastian picked it up and quickly read through the data.

"What is this conductivity study from?" The patronizing old man was gone. Neil heard the driven CEO.

"From this and other rocks like it." Neil picked a specimen jar out of his bag and placed it on the desk.

"This would …." Sebastian trailed off.

"Revolutionize clean energy in the world."

"You want to sell this to me to save your company. Why would I do that?"

"I'm offering Finn Technical a stake in Otherworld."

"You know that means you'd have to answer to me." Sebastian's revealed his teeth.

"I know, but we've exhausted our resources and it's the only way to get her back."

"Her?" Sebastian cocked his head to the side and Neil's eyes widened at his slip.

"Dr. Jane Sawyer, my partner in this endeavor, led the expedition and is trapped with a few others on the other side." Neil stumbled.

"Is she why you visited the safety deposit box for your

mother's ring?"

"You knew about that?"

"I keep tabs when someone visits that box."

"Yes, she is." Neil admitted and reached inside his bag for a couple of flash drives and other folders. Sebastian stood and crossed the room and poured two glasses of bourbon from his glass decanter. He handed one to Neil.

"You wear this well son."

"What do you mean?"

"Caring about someone more than yourself." Sebastian sipped his drink. "You did well bringing this to me. I think this is an investment we can make. Others will verify your data, but I think they'll agree with my understanding."

"You tend to get your way."

"So, how about a seventy-thirty split on revenue once we make the investment to fix your machine?"

"What?"

"This is a negotiation, son. Seventy-thirty splits since we are incurring the up-front investment."

"Fifty-fifty and Otherworld controls the patents on the technologies developed using the material."

"Sixty-forty and You control the patents."

"Deal."

"Well done, son."

"That was suspiciously easy." Neil took a sip.

"Cornelius, I'm old. Legacy matters to me." Sebastian paused, "I've wanted you to succeed me here at Finn Technical. Carry the mantle, but I couldn't just hand it to you. You had to earn it."

"I didn't want your handout."

"I know, but this," Sebastian gestured at the rock and the files of data, "is a discovery all your own. You'll be the highest preforming section of Finn Technical by a mile. There won't be any question to who my successor should be."

Neil looked up at the knock on his office door. "Come in." Dana opened the door and entered. Neil sighed.

"Expecting someone else."

"If Jeremy from Finn Technical comes to my office one more time I'm going to punch him." Neil leaned back in his chair and asked, "What can I do for you?"

"Just thought you'd want to go over the control room, so you're good to go for mission control tomorrow." Dana put her hand on the edge of the sofa in his office.

Neil turned his head to the side. "You're running

mission control tomorrow."

"I thought I'd be leading the expedition."

"No, I will."

"Neil, what if something goes wrong?"

"You'll be more useful than I will. They'll need the only other person who knows this machine as intimately as Jane did."

"Are you sure?" Dr. Prewitt sat down.

"Yeah, I am. She dropped into my life and kept coming. This time I have to go after her."

"Fair enough. See you in the morning."

"Get some sleep, Dana." Neil wouldn't sleep all night. The ring in his pocket reminded him of what he was doing all this for.

The tunnel of lights spun faster and faster. Neil focused on the empty section of wall on the far side. Motion Sickness had to be prevented when you were wearing a contained environmental suit. A crack resounded in the room and the blank space of wall was gone and all Neil could see was a rocky terrain with what looked like a stick with a flag on it.

"Team deploying," Neil said.

"Acknowledged. Good Luck," Dana said in the coms.

Neil and the three other members of the away team moved forward into the portal. They walked out into the rocky hills. A flag from their survival kits waved in the wind. The sky was brighter than they anticipated lit by twin suns.

"Everyone in," Neil asked. Affirmatives filled his earpiece. He turned and saw the lab floating in the hole in the sky. "Johnson, do you have a signal on their trackers?"

"The signal frequencies aren't working. I'll try to recalibrate now that we are all in the same area." Johnson twiddled with the communication controls in front of him.

"Mr. Finn," Abby Spencer said.

"Yeah Spencer?" Neil turned towards her.

"Can't we just follow the flags?" She pointed behind Neil.

Neil turned and shielded his eyes and saw waving about two hundred meters away another flag waving in the wind. "Good point. Johnson keep working on the signal, but we are heading towards those flags." Good job Jane. The crew headed out. Neil in front and Abby Spencer behind him. Johnson stood beside her as he twiddled his communication dials. Robert Landover was last in the formation carrying a large assault rifle. The military protection of the bunch.

The gravity was heavier here. Neil felt it pull with each step as they climbed up the rocky hill. Neil's lungs guzzled air as they labored against the gravity. They stopped at the flag and Neil asked, "Everyone ok?" The three other team members gave a thumbs up sign. "Good, just remember the gravity and if you feel weird call it out."

They pushed towards the next flag over by a cave and climbed up a rocky path. The rocks that his father had moved heaven and Earth to get more of were everywhere here. An embarrassment of riches. "Any sign of them, Johnson?"

"Not yet. I can't get a signal."

"Think they are in that cave, Robert?" Neil asked.

"Likely. Defensible and shelter from this sun." Robert huffed and puffed as he spoke the gravity affected them all. Neil's muscles protested the gravity on the climb. They arrived at the cave.

"I'll go first. Switch on your lights and let's go." The other members of the party followed instructions and entered the cave. There was still no sign of the group left behind at the mouth of the cave. The walls were smooth and well worn. Their coms crackled and a familiar voice broken in.

"Mission Control, this is Jane Sawyer. Come in."

"Jane," Neil said. He couldn't stop himself from speaking.

"Neil?" Jane's voice filled with emotion.

"Yeah, we're here. Are you in the cave?" Neil saw them in the cave. The team sprinted towards their lost comrades. Neil embraced Jane.

"You came." She whispered.

"Always. I'd cross the universe for you."

Jarrod K Williams is a speculative fiction author currently residing in the Midwest with his wife and two children. When not reading or writing speculative fiction he is an avid Cleveland sports fan. His work has previously appeared in *Small Shifts: Short Stories of Fantastical Transformation* from Lintusen Press.

FOR GORDIE

Philip Mann

T+ 01-12-55

(Time of launch , day, hour, minute)

One day past launch, and we're halfway to lunar orbit. The target is not the moon, it's way beyond that. For the record, and in case anything goes wrong, I'll introduce myself and my crew.

I'm Astrid and I captain of this crew.

Mason is the chief scientist and he has to know everything that goes into this ship, the chemistry, the reactions, the payload, he has to know what is planned and what isn't planned. He has to know the unknowns. He also knows the course and everything about navigation that has ever been known.

Gordon, or Gordie as he insists we call him is the

engineer. He could probably build us an engine out of scrap metal if I asked him to. He can calculate the thrust of a given volume of fuel down to the molecule.

Bobbie is the crew psychologist. I never understood why we need a shrink on board, we've all been through endless tests and evaluations. Such are our orders, such is my duty.

Sandra, or Sandy is our botanist, agricultural expert. Farmer in plain lingo. She can grow anything we need short of an Angus bull, which is a pity, if you ask me. But we have seeds and grafts to survive all sorts of conditions, for an extended period. This will be a long haul.

We're going to Mars.

T+03-04-28

In half an hour we'll commence the boost period. This ship, the Drake, will use the lunar gravitational pull to get into position, and then our rockets will fire to put us on track to Mars. I'm supposed to be calm and in control, but this has to be the most galvanizing command I'll ever have to give. This is the first step outside Earth or lunar gravity. A first.

T+03-05-02

Ten seconds of power is all we need. We shut it down and leave it quiet until we...

T+03-05-13

Not shutting down.

T+03-06-59

Still powering. Not good, could be a disaster. Fuel issue.

T+ 03-07-02

I order a shut-down of all power until he gets to the bottom of this. We have our suits on, oxygen still works. We're okay.

For now. Gordie calculates we went through about half our fuel supply and are off track from Mars. Mason made some calculations, says we're way past normal speed and on course to go through the asteroid belt. With a bit of luck, we won't hit anything.

T+03-08-00

Gordie found the problem, took care of it. We have normal functions now, lights, pressure, some heat. Fuel will be a problem, though. We burned through half of it, and we still have to get near a gravitational field, break out of it, get back to Earth somehow. And we're just starting our voyage.

T+07-06-39

Bobbie is talking to us, one by one. Might be a good idea, after all. Nobody has said it out loud, but we're in quite a pickle. We have no idea no solid idea of where we're headed, how to get home, how we can survive. I'm the captain, and it's my job to keep a tight lid on how I feel. If I fall apart, we're done for.

Mason spoke. He's usually quiet, so when he speaks it's important. He said we have some options. Our fuel is hydrogen peroxide. We know that. But that includes the option of using it for breathable oxygen It can be converted, and he's done it many times before. It's a two-way street. We can get more fuel, and we shouldn't need too much more than we have now, but that cuts down on oxygen.

Or we can use that oxygen as a fuel, if we need a powerful blast. He looked at me, and said it's my call. I looked around my crew, taking stock. Sandy had something to say.

She said that we had a lot of space to grow what we need, and she could use waste matter as soil and fertilizer. Bobbie asked if that meant we would be growing beans, eating them, doing our business, and getting into some endless cycle. The crew stared snickering and Gordie and the boys got into silly jokes. I smiled and shook my head. We were in a major crisis, and we needed a break. Gordon gets serious and asks

Mason something about our payload, and the experiments on board. They look at each other. Something is going on, and I knew what it was.

One of the experiments we were to conduct concerned the nature of Mars, its density, makeup and other calculations. The payload was a series of explosives. Big explosives, too. Nuclear. They packed a punch. It would be difficult, but the two of them, Gordie and Mason, might be able to turn the explosives into some sort of rocket. A very powerful booster that might get us back home, sooner or later. Or blow us all to bits.

I asked Mason, where are we headed now, as closely as he could predict? He said, if we make it through the asteroid belt, which is not a guaranteed thing, then we should get within two days sailing – he liked using nautical terms- of Jupiter. Close enough to see the moons. He looked at me and the others, and I knew he had something in his mind.

We have the ability to get close to the moons, especially Europa. It has an ice cover, and underneath may be water. Liquid water. It may have life, people. Living things beyond Earth. And it would be us, Bobbie, Mason, Sandy, him, and me. Astrid. Captain of the USS Drake.

The crew was electrified. He was saying that this crew had an outside chance of going down in history. We could be on the edge of immortality.

I asked how long until we reached that point. Mason said that normally it would take six years. But that malfunction had given us an enormous boost. We would reach it, all things being equal, in four months.

Bobbie pointed out that if everything we really equal, we wouldn't be where we were in the first place. Then she got into a rant of sorts, something like a standup comic. It got raunchy, but it lifted the mood.

This was totally against protocol, but the crew needed it. We knew what we were up against. The odds were very long against our getting home, or to anywhere. We had to make the best of it. I asked Gordie what he had to say.

He said, yes, the odds were long. We were already out of lunar gravitational field, and going almost ten times the engineered speed. Just to slow down would take fuel, and we were getting to the point where communications with Central would be impractical. A fifteen-minute delay and getting longer. We were on our own.

Sandy told us that between the food supplies we had on board and the yields we would get by growing new legumes, we could manage well. It was feasible. The problem, as Bobbie told us, was mental. How we would put up with each other. As she said, we could really get on each other's nerves.

I summarized for the crew. Going back to Earth might be possible, and Gordie could do it. But it was a long shot. We would have to put on the brakes, so to speak, and turn around. And it might not work.

We could continue where we were going and hope not to be clobbered by an asteroid or random hazard. No sure thing there either.

Or we could set a course for just a smidgen outside of Jupiter (I do get unscientific at times) and try to get some data about Europa. I was giving away how I felt, I know. But this was the idea of turning a disaster of a voyage into something never done before. And maybe not done for decades to yet come.

I looked around. Mason and Gordie were in. It was in their nature, they were always talking about explorers. Now they had the chance.

Bobbie saw the chance to go down in the history in her own profession, writing about a one-way trip to somewhere out there. Everything we did would be communicated back to Central. They would understand what we did, why we did it. It may take days or months.

Or years.

Sandy was excited in her own way. She would be the first astronaut farmer. She was sorry she hadn't packed a straw hat.

And I would be the captain. Captain of the USS Drake. Hundreds of years from now, all our names would be remembered.

We set about our tasks, our calculations. I looked around at the crew, on the sly.

They were each lost in their thoughts. For all our bravado and gung-ho talk, we were scared. But we hung together. We were giving each other a chance, and no one would take it away.

T+120-05-30

We're within sight of Jupiter. It's about as big as a dime, visible to the naked eye. The crew has settled into its duties, and there's something else.

Mason and Bobbie are getting friendly with each other. They manage to be apart from everybody else certain times of day, or what we call day. We all have to do what we can to stay sane, as long as the crew is not endangered in any way.

T+120 07-32

Sandy had a discussion with Gordie, something to do with farming, creating a matrix for soil and then crops. They get along well, I see. Very well indeed.

T+122-08-00

Bobbie got up before the others, talked with me a while. She has something on her mind. I had a feeling about her for a long time, and now she confirmed it.

T+123-08-01

Bobbie asked me something about activities, trying to keep the crew content, or at least not suicidal. Good point.

T+124-08-00

Bobbie wanted my opinion on relationships in the group. She was talking about sex in this long-term voyage. I saw this coming back in training. I hope it works out, we have a long way to go. Maybe a lifetime.

T+125-08-11

Bobbie stopped by after the rest of the crew was asleep.

T+125-08-12

Private note. Bobbie.

T+125-09-06

I didn't think this could happen to me. I lead a private life, as private as you can be in a NASA training program. But

Bobbie has me pegged.

T+125-09-12

I had to address the crew. We're all looking at each other differently now. I'll be frank. Every single one of us is having sex with some other member. The men, the women, I'm afraid to think what will happen when rivalries turn confrontational and violent. This is a small group, we all know what everybody else is doing, and with whom.

T+126-07-01

Gordie wants permission to adjust the explosive charge on one of the probes. He says it's a mini nuclear device, and could be useful if we want to ever get back home. I gave him permission. Who knows what will happen to us anyway. He seems to be the only one not interested in sex or any human bond. Maybe that's why he qualified for this crew.

T+130-01-20

Bobbie stopped by again after the crew was asleep. She's good company.

T+135-03-23

We're within range of Europa, and launched a probe. It

succeeded far beyond our expectations, and we have enough samples to write entire volumes, and raise new questions about the nature of life.

After some testing, Mason determined that the water is safe to drink. We can do an enormous number of things with this prize, including drink, refresh our oxygen supply, and just look at it. Fresh water after four months in space!

T+136-02-00

Gordie says it's time to test his rocket. The calculations are sound, he, Mason and I went through them, and the boost will send us on course for home.

The crew is subdued by the news. I'm surprised. Maybe they liked the isolation, the idea of being in their own world. But they soon understood that while this was not viable in the long term.

T+136-03-30

We're lucky to have survived the boost. Gordie calculated it well, modelling it after the Space Shuttle booster rockets. WE all felt as if we were being crushed into the walls of this craft. But after a few seconds, he gave me the thumbs up. We're on course for home.

T+140-01-10

Gordie's radioactive. He worked on those charges without protection, said he had to, given the lack of anything suitable. He won't make it back.

T+150-09-10

Gordie died this morning as a result of radiation poisoning. We tethered his body to the outside of the craft, and we'll bring him abord just before reentry, so he doesn't burn up.

We survived because of him.

So this voyage and all of its discoveries are his. He got us out there and back.

For you, Gordie. For you.

Philip Mann lives in Montreal with his wife and several characters of his Dark Muse series, a work that combines the paranormal, romance and Jewish mysticism. If he had a dog, he would be a cat person.

THE CHALLENGE

J. Paul Cooper

Francine had been dozing off, but woke up when the bus stopped. The driver explained no traffic was permitted near the park that bordered on Stonelake Boulevard and 47th Street.

Stepping off the bus, Francine considered texting her husband George to see if he'd started making supper, but decided it wasn't worth it. George would be busy writing the latest entry for his blog, a serialized story that he intended to self-publish as a novel. It would be better if he was actually making money writing, but when he was absorbed in his fictional world, at least he wasn't whining about how much he hated his warehouse job.

After a grueling ten-hour shift at the mall, Francine

was exhausted and in no mood to cook. She decided to order pizza. When the food arrived, she'd watch a movie undisturbed, while George continued writing.

Francine could see police vehicles blocking the entrance to the park, their lights flashing. At first she thought it might have been a murder scene, but then a pair of military helicopters flew overhead. Why was the miliary involved?

Francine decided to walk towards the park, as it wasn't far from home. It was odd; some people were straining to see beyond the police barrier, while others were running away terrified.

Francine joined the crowd, staring at a vessel resting among the trees. She had seen enough sci fi movies to guess that it was probably too large to be a shuttle, but too small to be a battle cruiser.

She started searching for her husband among the throng of onlookers, then realized he might not know about the "arrival." George often listened to Classic Rock at an ear-splitting volume while he was writing. If he had the television turned off, he might be completely oblivious to the historical events unfolding near their house.

The crowd went silent, and the police and military raised their weapons, as a ramp extended from the vessel. A tall alien stepped out, peering at the humans assembled around his ship. "I am Yarat!"

The crowd cheered and clapped. The alien ignored them and called out louder, "I am here to accept the challenge from George, Slayer of the Unclean!"

Francine turned to another woman standing nearby. "Did that alien just say, 'George, Slayer of the Unclean?'"

The woman shrugged. "That's what it sounded like."

Francine raced towards home, glad that she was wearing comfortable walking shoes. A few minutes later she slammed the front door behind her.

George was standing in the kitchen holding a cup of coffee in one hand, and headphones in the other. He had changed from his work clothes into sweat pants and a T-shirt. George stood about five foot, ten inches, and he was in reasonably good shape, but he wasn't the kind of guy you'd hire for a gladiator movie.

"Hi. You all right?" he asked.

"Yeah, fine." Francine answered as she gasped for breath.

"What's up with all the sirens?"

"No time to explain," replied Francine, "we need to talk about your blog."

"Sorry," George said, "I was supposed to make supper. You know how I get when I'm writing; I lose track of time. I'll clean the house tomorrow."

Normally she'd appreciate the help, but today it didn't matter. "Believe me George, cooking supper, cleaning the house, none of that is important right now."

"What's going on?"

Ignoring his question, Francine walked over to the living room window, pulling back the drapes. "Are you expecting someone?" asked George.

Francine turned to her husband. "You've been hiding something from me George. You've been receiving threats."

"What are you talking about?"

"It's something to do with your blog. What was the last thing you wrote about?"

"I wrote about the beautiful Francine of course."

Francine walked over and kissed him. George wasn't very romantic, but naming the most gorgeous vixen in the universe after her, was a good start. "What did you write about the beautiful Francine?"

"Well...."

"You need to hurry George."

"The condensed version...."

"Yes."

"Yarat the Unblessed has kidnapped Francine, so George sends him a message, 'I, George, Slayer of the Unclean, do challenge Yarat the Unblessed to fight to the death for the hand of Francine. She is the one, who is unequalled in beauty among the stars.'"

"And someone answered that challenge."

George shrugged. "Well, someone claiming to be Yarat the Unblessed sent me a message. He said it was me who was going to be slayed. It's nothing to worry about, must be a member from my writers' group, you know, role-playing."

"It's not someone from your writers' group."

"What makes you say that?"

"The Universe is a big place, George. Did it ever occur to you that, if there really are aliens out there, that there might be someone called Yarat?"

"That's crazy, there's no one out there called Yarat."

"Oh yes there is George. And guess what? He's here, and he's looking for you."

Yarat stood six foot, seven inches tall and looked surprisingly human-like. Other than his light green skin there was nothing about him that was frighteningly alien. He had six fingers, but they weren't abnormally long. His hair was light brown and weaved together, flowing down his back.

The alien rolled his shoulders and stretched his neck, as he marched to where George, Slayer of the Unclean had issued the challenge. He had expected George to be waiting from him, ready to fight to the death as soon as he stepped off his vessel, but George hadn't appeared. Yarat was confused, nothing about this world was as it had been described. George, Slayer of the Unclean was supposed to live in a castle, but there were no castles here. Perhaps George was some peasant, pretending to be a nobleman. That alone, deserved death.

A dozen heavily armed police officers followed the alien, their weapons drawn. Military helicopters circled overhead, anti-tank missiles and heavy machine guns at the ready. The police and military personnel had been warned not to antagonize the visitor. He didn't appear to have any weapons, other than the long blade strapped to his back, but no one knew if he was alone. The vessel in the park might hold other aliens. There might even be an alien fleet, ready to annihilate the human race on his command.

George and Francine waited for the alien. There was no point in hiding, if he could pinpoint where the blog had been sent from, it would be a waste of time. He stopped in front of them. "I am Yarat."

It looked like Yarat was wearing a kilt made of reptile skin. The garment covering his upper body resembled a hockey jersey made of finely woven gold rings. With broad shoulders and flat gut, he wouldn't have looked out of place on the cover of a romance novel.

George cleared his throat. "We come in peace."

Francine glanced at her husband.

George shrugged. "You got something better?"

"You sent out the challenge?" Yarat demanded. "You are George, Slayer of the Unclean?"

The alien wore a glowing medallion and Francine guessed it was some kind of translator. She smiled, trying to appear relaxed. "I'm Francine." She pointed at her husband. "George, my husband writes stories. He doesn't slay anyone."

Yarat stared at George, appraising the puny human. He crushed an ant with the heel of a boot. "I don't think George could slay one of these."

"Like my wife Francine said," George replied, "I'm a writer, I tell stories."

The alien smiled at Francine. "George, Slayer of Nothing tells many lies, but what he wrote about Francine is true. She is a pleasure to behold. I have travelled to the far reaches of the stars and she is the most beautiful female I have ever seen."

The alien turned towards George. "Your challenge may not been real, but this one is! Yarat challenges George, Slayer of Nothing, for the hand of the exquisite Francine. A fight to the death!"

It was obvious to Francine, that there was no way George was going to survive a fight with Yarat. She wondered what would happen if George refused to fight. Would Yarat kill him for being a coward? Perhaps, she could talk the alien out of fighting.

"Although I appreciate the compliment," Francine began, "I won't always look as good as I do now. It wouldn't be fair to you, if thirty years from now, you weren't happy with the bargain. And besides, I have responsibilities. My boss relies on me at the store, I'm kind of a servant."

Yarat turned to Francine. "A servant? If you come with Yarat, you will never be a servant again, for you will be my queen and live in a palace. You will be the one who is served. And on my planet, you will never grow old. Yarat has lived a thousand of your years. Do I look old?"

"Not really," Francine replied.

"On my world," Yarat continued, "the air is clear, the oceans are clean, and we don't use poison on our crops."

Yarat glared at George. "It is time, George, Slayer of

Nothing. Prepare to die."

The police raised their weapons.

Yarat glanced at the police and smiled. "I can destroy one human, or I can destroy all humans. The choice is yours."

Francine's heart raced. Yarat was about to kill George, and perhaps the entire human race, and she was the only one who could stop it.

Yarat reached for his blade. Francine stepped forward and grasped his arm. "There's no need to kill. If I go with you, will you spare George's life? Will that satisfy your challenge?"

"Yarat will spare his life."

"And the lives of all humans?"

The alien looked up at the military helicopters. "As long as they don't use their weapons."

"Then, we have an agreement."

"We have an agreement," answered Yarat, "but you must come with me now."

George stared in disbelief. "You can't do this."

Tears streamed down Francine's face, as she held her husband's hands in hers. "What choice do I have? He'll destroy everything."

"Will you ever come back?" George asked.

Francine kissed him gently on the lips. "No."

It had been a hundred Earth years since Queen Francine, "The One Whose Beauty Outshines the Stars," had come from a distant galaxy to reign with King Yarat. There would be a great celebration and the Queen wanted a new dress. Francine could have asked a dressmaker to come to the palace, but she liked to visit the markets. Yarat had gone on a hunting trip, and she had some free time to spend as she wished. If was a relief to have a day free of official duties.

Yarat's world was indeed peaceful, but it was no democratic utopia. His power was absolute and unchallenged. It was a strange mix of advanced technology and rural tranquility. You could fly by shuttle throughout the countryside, and buy fresh produce from villagers who used primitive farming techniques. The palace had ancient stone walls on the outside, but modern conveniences inside.

Preparing to leave the palace, Francine took a moment to check her hair in a mirror. Just like Yarat had promised, she looked just as good as she had when she left Earth. In fact, living in the pristine environment, she looked even better.

Francine smiled as she wondered how she'd answer, if a reporter asked her about life with King Yarat. " If you think someone can get on your nerves after you've been married for four or five years, just image how they can get on your nerves after a hundred years!"

Francine boarded a shuttle, flying to a village near the palace. As usual, she was accompanied by armed guards. She would have enjoyed walking through the village by herself, but the Queen had to follow security protocol, even when visiting her favourite shops.

A few minutes later, Francine moved through the aisles of a dress shop, touching the finely woven fabrics. As she did, the enticing aroma from the local bakery drifted through open shop windows. Francine paused, as a distant memory returned. She smiled at the shop owner, "Well, I guess it's too late now."

"Nothing is too late for Queen Francine," the shop owner replied. "Whatever you want, I can have it ready by tomorrow morning."

"Oh, I wasn't talking about a dress," Francine said. "I just remembered what I was thinking about, when I got off the bus."

Francine noticed the puzzled looked on the shop owner's face. "I forgot to order the pizza."

J. Paul Cooper has a Bachelor of Arts (Political Science.) His articles, short stories and essays have been published in magazines, literary journals, print anthologies, and newspapers. He has also self-published three eBooks and written several unproduced screenplays.

OTHER SHORT STORY COLLECTIONS FROM LINTUSEN PRESS

SMALL SHIFTS: short stories of fantastical transformation

Not all shifters turn into magnificent beasts. Sure there are those humans who transform into wolves and bears, but this book is about the smaller creatures. Learn about the trials and tribulations of folks who turn into raccoons, hamsters, mosquitoes, or bumblebees. 11 delightful tales of Small Shifts.

THE DRABBLE ADVENT CALENDAR

A drabble is a story of precisely one hundred words. Here are 25 family friendly winter themed drabbles; one perfect tidbit of story to savour each day leading up to Christmas.